MEASLE
and the
WRATHMONK

MEASLE
and the
WRATHMONK

IAN OGILVY

SCHOLASTIC INC.
New York Toronto London Auckland Sydney
Mexico City New Delhi Hong Kong Buenos Aires

Thanks to Kitty, Sam and Lee,
for some superlative suggestions

ISBN 0-439-79791-8

Copyright © 2004 by Ian Ogilvy. All rights reserved.
Published by Scholastic Inc., 557 Broadway, New York, NY
10012, by arrangement with HarperCollins Publishers.
SCHOLASTIC and associated logos are trademarks and/or
registered trademarks of Scholastic Inc.

12 11 10 9 8 7 6 5 4 3 2 1   5 6 7 8 9 10/0

Printed in the U.S.A.   40

First Scholastic printing, September 2005

Typography by Amy Ryan

For Barnaby and Matilda

CONTENTS

MEASLE
and the
WRATHMONK

1

THE
HORRIBLE HOUSE

Measle Stubbs was ten and a half years old. He was small, thin and bony. He had a short snub nose, a pair of eyes colored a deep emerald green and (when he felt like it) a wide and friendly smile. His hair was brown and stood up all over his head in spiky tufts. It was the oddest haircut—long where it should have been short, short where it should have been long—and the reason it was like this was because Measle cut his hair himself, using a blunt and rusty kitchen knife, with which he sawed and hacked at his hair whenever it got so long that it fell in his eyes. Apart from having the most uneven haircut imaginable, his hair also hadn't been washed in a very long time. Neither had his clothes, and sometimes he smelled pretty bad, particularly when the weather was warm. It wasn't warm very often where Measle Stubbs lived, because he lived in a cold and horrible house.

The horrible house was at the far end of a dreary, dirty street full of dreary, dirty houses, but three things set it apart from all the others. The first was the way it looked—all black, with a tall, pointed roof, tall, dark, narrow windows like blind eyes and tall, soot-caked chimneys that were like dirty fingers pointing at the sky. It looked like something bad had happened in it—and, quite possibly, something bad could happen in it again tomorrow.

The second thing was that it was the only house that was occupied. All the other houses had been deserted by their owners long ago and their doors and windows boarded over.

The third thing was also the strangest: all day and all night, winter, summer, autumn and spring, there was a small, black cloud that hung, never moving, over the dismal roof, dribbling a steady, constant stream of rain that fell only on the house where Measle Stubbs lived and not at all on any of the others in the street.

The house belonged to Basil Tramplebone, and Basil Tramplebone was Measle Stubbs's legal guardian. Measle lived in the house with just his legal guardian for company, and his legal guardian wasn't good company at all. He was very tall and thin and he always wore black clothes. A black coat and a black shirt and a black tie; black trousers and black socks and black shoes. His greasy hair was black, and he parted it in the middle and plastered it down on his head with black shoe polish. The only things that weren't black about him were his face and his hands: Basil's face was very white, as though all the blood had been drained out and replaced with milk. His eyes were like fish eyes—staring and blank and very, very cold. His long, bony hands were the color of candles, and the skin was so dry that it rustled when he rubbed his palms together, which he did when he was pleased. Basil Tramplebone wasn't pleased very often, so the rustling noise didn't happen very often.

If the outside of Basil Tramplebone's house was grim

and gloomy and depressingly ugly, the inside was even worse. All the rooms in the house smelled bad—each one in a different way—and most of them frightened Measle half to death. He certainly didn't dare go into the room that was supposed to be his bedroom. There was a huge black oak wardrobe in there, full of clothes that weren't his. They felt damp and smelled of mildew. Once Measle had gotten up enough courage to sort through the clothes. He stopped when he found the jacket. It was made of some sort of rough material and it had *three* sleeves—two in the usual places and a third that stuck out at the back. When he finally got up the courage to ask Basil about it, Basil told him to mind his own business—but if he *must* know, all the clothes in the wardrobe had been left there over the years by visiting friends of his, some of whom were, perhaps, a little *different*.

The wardrobe was in one dark corner of the bedroom, and a great, black bed that looked like a coffin was in the other. There were black velvet curtains over the windows and the glass in the windows was painted black, so you couldn't see out at all. What with the black painted walls and ceiling and floorboards, it was one of the gloomiest rooms you can imagine, and one that would certainly give you nightmares if you tried to sleep in it—so Measle didn't try at all. Instead, he slept on a pile of old rags in the kitchen, right up by the ancient iron stove, which was the only place in that horrible house that was at all warm.

Measle hated Basil Tramplebone and, of course, Basil Tramplebone hated Measle, because Basil hated everybody. He only looked after Measle because Measle's mother and father had been killed by an encounter with a deadly snake when Measle was four years old, leaving poor little Measle an orphan.

The story about the deadly snake had come from Basil who, in Measle's experience, always told the truth. His parents had left a lot of money in the bank and now it was all Measle's, but a judge had said that Measle was too young to have control of all that money and to live by himself and had appointed Basil—who said he was Measle Stubbs's fourth cousin twelve times removed and, therefore, Measle's closest living relative—to look after him and his money. The odd thing was that the judge had looked a little like Basil. The same black clothes, the same cold, fishy eyes, the same white, white face. He'd even talked a bit like Basil, too—and every time he'd looked at Basil, he'd smiled like a crocodile, as if he was approving of everything that Basil said.

There were only three rooms in the house that Measle could bear to be in—the bathroom, the kitchen and the attic. The bathroom smelled bad and the water that came out of the taps was brown, with green floating bits in it, so Measle didn't bathe very often. But at least there was a window in the bathroom, and sometimes Measle would stand on the cracked toilet seat and look out of the window at the dismal rail yards that were behind the house and dream of living somewhere else.

The kitchen was warm and dry, but it smelled of rotten cabbages and was infested with enormous cockroaches. Some of them were so big that when Measle stepped on them, they didn't go *crunch* under his foot like the smaller ones did. They simply wriggled about in a disgusting way until Measle took his foot off them and then they scuttled away under the stove, quite unharmed.

As for the attic, Measle had only recently been in it, because Basil had never allowed him to go up there before. *Something* interesting had certainly been going on up that narrow flight of stairs, because Basil spent many hours in the attic. For a long time Measle used to stand at the bottom of the stairs and listen—and occasionally he'd heard sounds that he couldn't explain to himself. And then one day, about six months ago, Basil had said, "Come with me, Measle," and he'd led the way up the cramped, steep staircase and into the extraordinary attic room—and Measle's jaw had dropped in amazement at what he saw.

It was the biggest—and probably the best—miniature railway set in the world.

From that moment, the attic became the one room in the house that Measle actually didn't mind spending time in. It was still a scary room; there was something in there that lived up in the rafters. Measle had seen movement among the dark beams of wood and once a pair of red, glowing eyes. What the something was, Measle didn't really want to know—just so long as it stayed out of sight. At least there were no cockroaches in the attic. In fact, there were no insects of any kind up there, which was odd because the rest of the house was crawling with them.

Measle was fascinated by the train set. Somehow Basil had managed to build a miniature version of the dismal rail yards on a huge table, right in the middle of the attic. The table was so big that there was only a narrow gap all the way around between its edge and the attic walls. It was a good thing that both Measle and Basil were so thin—otherwise they could never have fit in the sliver of space. Everything on the enormous table looked accurate, down to the smallest detail. The coal yard had a mound of tiny chips of real coal, the streetlights shone with a sickly yellow light and there was a constant, tiny stream of dirty water flowing in the miniature gutters. Farther out, away from the town, Basil had created a forest of tall pines, with the trees set so close together it was hard to see between them. It was very dark and gloomy, with strange little houses dotting the clearings in the woods. Those houses were quite different from the grimy ones around the rail yards. They were made of little logs, with stone chimneys and porches on the front, and Measle decided that, if he were an inhabitant of the place, he'd much rather live in one of them than in the depressing town houses.

Then there were the trains. From the moment he was allowed to watch Basil, it was obvious to Measle that Basil didn't care for anything modern. There were no electric commuter trains, no long-distance diesel trains. Everything about the set was old-fashioned, and all the locomotives were steam engines from an age long past. There were two sorts of trains, passenger trains and freight trains, and each one was detailed to the smallest degree. Every time Measle came to watch, he saw something new in the scenery. One day he saw that Basil had made a little plume of smoke come from the chimney of one of the houses in the woods. Another time, Basil had built a water tower by the side of the tracks, and when one of the freight trains stopped underneath it, the tower let out a tiny trickle of water that filled the boiler of the engine. Once Measle noticed that Basil had added a lake in the middle of the forest—not made of real water, but a mirror embedded in the surface, surrounded by the little pine trees.

Measle had to admit that Basil was good with his hands. It seemed as though Basil could make just about anything, so long as the thing was very small. Sometimes Measle was amazed at the details of all the scaled-down objects—every window in the houses looked like real glass, every leaf on the trees looked as if it would drop off when autumn came and every worn paving stone on the dirty pavements looked as if it had been trodden on by countless shuffling feet.

There were quite a few people in the model, too. The painted plastic figures were positioned about the train set, doing all the things that people usually do: shopping, gossiping on street corners, standing on station platforms waiting for trains. There were a few animals as well—a little black-and-white dog sniffing around a lamppost, a cat lounging on a windowsill and, deep in the forest, a family of three black bears walking in a line near the lake.

When Basil played with his trains, he always ate a whole box of glazed doughnuts and drank a gallon of pink lemonade out of a plastic jug, and some of the crumbs and some of the sugar and an occasional drop of lemonade would fall onto the tabletop. Measle never got a doughnut or a glass of lemonade because Basil never offered him any and Measle didn't dare ask.

Measle would stare at the crumbs, hoping that Basil would need to go to the bathroom, because while he was gone Measle might be able to sneak over and lick his finger and dab up the crumbs and the sugar and eat them. But Basil never seemed to go to the bathroom at all, even after eating a whole box of glazed doughnuts and drinking a gallon of pink lemonade, so Measle never got the chance.

Now, Measle knew that Basil was spending money—*Measle's* money—on the train set. Basil didn't seem to work at a real job and the only person he ever called was the banker Measle's parents had used. Measle didn't mind so much about the money spent on the train set, because it was probably the best train set in the world and he liked looking at it. But he thought it was totally unfair that he never got to play with the train set himself. He could only watch Basil play with it, and he could only watch when Basil invited him.

One night, while Measle lay curled tight up against the stove, an idea came to him. He was awake because the cockroaches were having a party—or what sounded like a party, if cockroaches had them—under the stove. There was a lot of clicking and rustling and *tap-tap-tap*ping of cockroach feet, and he couldn't sleep with all that noise going on, so he decided to think instead. That was when the idea came to him. It was a brilliant idea. It was also a dangerous idea, but the best ideas often are and Measle was prepared to take the risk.

The next day at lunch (Basil was having fried sausages and bacon and chips and ketchup, and Measle was having a piece of stale bread and a paper cup of water) Measle said, "Oh, Mr. Tramplebone, sir, the bank called this morning. They want to see you."

"The bank called?" said Basil. He stared at Measle with his cold fish eyes. "When?"

"While you were still asleep, sir." said Measle. "Something about some extra money."

"Money?"

"Yes. For us, of course. They want to see you about it. The man said something about investing it."

"Invesssting?" Basil always hissed like a rattlesnake whenever he said the letter *s*.

"Yes, Mr. Tramplebone. He said it was too much just to leave in an ordinary bank account."

"I shall telephone them."

"Yes, sir—but the trouble is, the telephone doesn't seem to be working anymore, sir."

"Not working?"

"No, sir."

The reason the telephone wasn't working anymore was because Measle had taken the plug out of the socket. He watched nervously as Basil tried the phone. Basil listened to the earpiece for a moment and then hissed like a snake.

"What a nuisssance." He put the receiver down. Then he put on his long black coat and picked up his long black umbrella, which looked like a sleeping vampire bat.

"I'm going out, Measle," he hissed. "To the bank. Behave yoursssself. Do nothing. Nothing at all."

Basil hardly ever went out. He had all their food delivered from the local supermarket and bought all the stuff for the train set from catalogs. In fact, when the door closed behind him, Measle realized that this was the first time he could remember ever being alone in the house and, for a moment, he felt scared. Then he said to himself, "What can a house do to you? It's not like it's a burglar or a murderer or anything, so what can

13

it possibly do to you?" That made him feel a little better.

He looked through a crack in the front door and watched Basil slither down the path to the street. A small piece of the black cloud that hung over the house detached itself and began to follow Basil. It dribbled a little shower of rain on Basil's open umbrella. At the end of the path, Basil turned right, which was the way to the better part of town, where the bank was. Basil was going to have to walk the whole way, because they didn't have a car and there were no buses that came out to this side of the railroad yards. The bank was about a mile and a half away, which meant that even with his long spider legs, Basil was going to be gone for some time.

It was enough time, Measle thought. More than enough time.

2

THE
TRAIN SET

Measle's brilliant idea was this: once he'd gotten Basil out of the house, he would climb up the stairs to the attic and sit down on Basil Tramplebone's special high stool and reach over and turn the master knob—the one that brought the train set to life—and then, well, he'd just sit there and play with the biggest and best train set in the entire world all by himself.

Of course, Measle's idea wasn't really all that brilliant. Basil would get to the bank and find out that there wasn't any extra money at all and that would make him completely furious, and when Basil Tramplebone was completely furious, Measle's life became even nastier than normal. But Measle didn't think of this, because he was so excited by the rest of the plan. The chance to play with Basil's train set without any interference was just too good to pass up.

Something else that was too good to pass up was the opportunity to eat something. Measle went quickly to the kitchen—it smelled even worse than usual—and opened the ancient refrigerator. He was hoping to find something nice, but there was nothing at all, except a paper bag full of old, wrinkled carrots down at the bottom in the vegetable tray. Measle didn't particularly like carrots, but he hadn't had one for such a long time that he'd forgotten what they tasted like, so he stuffed the paper bag into his pocket and headed for the staircase.

Measle raced up the creaking stairs, flight after flight, until he arrived, panting for breath, right at the top of the house. The attic door stood open. Measle went in and stared at the huge table. He carefully avoided looking up toward the rafters.

It had been a month since he was last allowed in

here; was there anything new? Measle looked all around the enormous table—yes, there were some changes. Not with the set itself; the tracks and the trains were all in their usual places and none of the buildings had been altered. But Basil had moved some of the model people around and he'd put several of them into some very odd situations. There, for instance, near the coal yards: a workman in a blue coat and a yellow plastic helmet was sitting on the edge of a rectangular hole in the pavement, his hands full of what appeared to be electrical cables. Obviously Basil wanted it to look like the man was making repairs to the main power supply. But that wasn't all Basil wanted to show, for standing directly behind this workman, unseen by him, was another figure of a man holding a bucket of water high in the air—and Measle saw that the bucket of water was about to be tipped over onto the workman!

Measle knew that water and electricity were a very dangerous combination.

Measle frowned. This was very odd. He looked over the train set again. What else was different? Ah—there, deep in the woods—the trio of bears were no longer strolling by the mirror lake. Now they were clustered around the base of a pine tree and all staring hungrily upward—and there, high in the branches, was the figure of a little girl, dressed as a Brownie, clinging tightly to the tree trunk! Measle looked further, his eyes stopping on the scene that was taking place in a siding near one of the stations. A group of people were bending over something on the railway tracks. He looked closer. The something was an old woman—and the people clustered around her were tying her down on the rails!

This is weird, thought Measle. Why had Basil decided that some of the people should be threatened like this? He started searching the train set again. There, in the town square, at the foot of the town hall steps—a figure of a woman, crouching in obvious terror, her fists pressed tightly over her eyes, so as to block out the sight of the huge Bengal tiger that was creeping steadily toward her!

Measle grinned. He couldn't help it. There was something quite funny about this. These poor people, all in such danger—but not really in any danger at all, of course, since everything was just plastic and nothing was real. Well, Basil had certainly made the train set even more fascinating than ever. Was there anything else to see? Oh yes, there—a round, fat little man with a shiny bald head, carrying what looked like a heavy suitcase, running as fast as his short legs could carry him down a street that led out toward the forest. Behind him, in close pursuit, was a small mob of people carrying banners and placards on sticks. Measle leaned closer, peering at the tiny writing on the placards. DOWN WITH KNOWLEDGE! was written on one and DEATH TO A SALESMAN! was on another.

Weirder and weirder, thought Measle.

Anything else? He'd covered the town pretty closely; what about the forest? Anything other than the Brownie and the bears? Oh yes! There, in a clearing of cut-down trees, a big black man was sitting on a tree stump. At his feet lay a canvas tool bag, and next to it a tiny chain saw and a red fuel can. The man's broad shoulders were slumped and his head hung low. There was a look of despair about him, and he seemed oblivious to the three figures creeping up behind him. The figures looked like lumberjacks. They were approaching him with great stealth, and all three were carrying axes raised over their heads.

For a moment, Measle wondered whether it might be fun to rescue all these poor people from their predicaments. He could put the bears back by the lake, he could throw the Bengal tiger out the attic window, he could untie the ropes that bound the old woman to the railway tracks—but no, that would be really stupid. Basil would get horribly angry if he messed with the layout. What he was about to do was bad enough, but perhaps he might get away with it just this once. But if he changed anything that Basil had set up so carefully, Basil would be sure to notice and then Measle would be in real trouble. Having made the decision, he squeezed through the narrow gap between the edge of the table and the wall, until he came to the control box.

The control box didn't look like the usual sort of electric train console; for a start, there weren't any plastic parts to it. The whole thing was made of black metal and all the knobs were black metal, too, and the knobs were larger than usual and had strange markings on them.

Measle climbed up onto Basil's tall stool. If he leaned

forward, he could just about reach all the knobs. He knew which one started up the power and which ones controlled the different sections of track, because he'd watched Basil carefully for a long time. He reached out and turned the big black knob on the left of the control panel, and there was a low hum as the power came on. So far, so good. Now, which train to start with?

The train Measle liked best was a little green freight train with a tall smokestack and two flatbed trucks that it pulled behind it. The flatbed trucks were loaded with tiny logs. The freight train ran on a particular section of track that took it around the edge of the table to a miniature logging mill, where miniature circular saws cut the miniature logs into miniature planks of wood. The little green freight train was Measle's favorite because it looked the friendliest of all the trains. It didn't seem quite as menacing as most of the others—particularly the biggest one of all, which was a grimy, oily monster locomotive, with a dented cowcatcher on the front and three dusty Pullman coaches behind.

So, the little green freight train it would be.

Measle put his hand on the third knob from the left

and gently turned it. On the other side of the table, the freight train started to move slowly down its section of track. Measle turned the knob a bit more, and the freight train picked up speed. It was moving away from him, toward the far end of the table. In a few seconds, it would make the long turn at the end of the table and chug toward him and its usual station—the logging mill, a few feet away from where he sat. He watched as it began to take the curve. He turned the knob a little more, and the wheels of the freight train began to spin faster.

Measle was concentrating so hard on what he was doing that he didn't see something that would have scared him badly. The monster locomotive, with its dented cowcatcher and its three Pullman coaches, had begun to move out of its siding and onto the main tracks. It did so quite silently and, at first, quite slowly—and, since Measle had his back to it, he didn't see or hear a thing.

The little freight train was now clattering down the long straight section of track on the very edge of the table. Measle decided to let it keep its speed up and stop it by the logging mill at the very last minute, which was something he'd seen Basil do lots of times. He watched intently as the freight train clicked and chuffed its way toward him. The track here was quite long and there was plenty of time to get ready for the stop. Then, out of the corner of his eye, Measle saw the monster locomotive.

It had joined the main track—the same one the freight train was on—and was now racing toward the smaller engine, its pistons flying, its smokestack belching and its oily wheels turning so fast that they seemed to blur. Measle gasped in horror. How could that have happened? He hadn't touched the knob that controlled the locomotive. Quickly—which one was the locomotive's controller? It was the fifth, wasn't it? Or was it the fourth? Measle reached for the fifth knob and turned it hard. Nothing happened. If anything, both trains seemed to speed up. Measle twisted the fourth knob and the two trains seemed to lean forward toward each other as they accelerated. He reached for both knobs and twisted them this way and that—and both knobs came away in his hands. Frantically, he tried to push them back onto their spindles but for some reason they wouldn't fit, so Measle grabbed the spindles themselves and tried to turn *them* but his fingers slipped on the oily metal and he couldn't get a proper grip. In desperation, he reached for the Power On knob. Measle grasped it with both hands and strained with all his strength.

The knob refused to budge.

A head-on collision was inevitable, and Measle was powerless to stop it.

"WHAT ISSS GOING ON?"

Measle whipped around on the tall stool, almost falling off in his fright. There in the doorway stood Basil Tramplebone. His fish eyes were staring and his long, bony fingers were clenched into fists and, for the first time ever, Measle saw a trace of red on each of Basil's chalky cheeks.

"WHAT HAVE YOU BEEN DOING?"

Measle tried to say something—anything—but his voice wouldn't work. His tongue felt swollen and his teeth felt numb and he didn't seem able to breathe. Behind him, he could hear the clatter as the two trains raced toward each other, but he couldn't turn and watch because Basil's fish eyes had pinned him in place.

Suddenly, Basil's gaze moved to the train set. Measle

saw Basil's eyes widen and the two angry spots of red disappear. Basil's whole face went a strange shade of gray, like a corpse's.

And then Basil did a very odd thing. He opened his mouth and said something. To Measle, it sounded a bit like *"Sssplzzxcffft gjriuvriok ssskargranglio!"*—a kind of snaky hiss, mixed with a kind of throat-clearing, mixed with a kind of teeth-grinding, mixed with a kind of nose-blowing sort of sound, which was as disgusting a noise as Measle had ever heard. At the same moment Basil was making this bloodcurdling noise, a strange glint of green flame appeared in his eyes, and a second later two very bright green beams of light, like twin lasers, suddenly shot out from his pupils. The beams missed Measle by an inch, zipping past his face with a sizzling sound and making the air near his nose smell of burned rubber. Measle cowered on the high stool, squeezed his eyes shut and put his hands over his ears, because Basil had never done anything like this before and Measle was suddenly very frightened indeed.

With his eyes tightly closed and his ears covered, Measle didn't hear the crash of the two trains. He didn't hear or see anything at all, and he began to wonder why nothing was happening. Even with his ears covered, it seemed to be awfully quiet. Surely Basil was going to hit him? But if so, why hadn't he done so already? What was going on? The seconds ticked by, and at last Measle's curiosity got the better of him and he cautiously opened his eyes.

And then he wished he hadn't.

Basil was standing very close to him and smiling. Measle had never seen Basil smile before. He hoped he never would again. It was ghastly. Usually, when people smile, the skin at the corners of their eyes wrinkles at the same time, which makes them look friendly. Basil's eyes didn't wrinkle at all. They stayed exactly the same as always, big and round and fishy—and very, very cold. His thin, pale lips were stretched wide, revealing a row of long, yellow teeth. The teeth at the sides of his mouth were even longer and they came to a sharp point. For a moment, Measle wondered if Basil might be a vampire. But surely vampires only had one set of pointed teeth—one on each side? Basil had *three* pointed teeth on each side, which made him look a bit like an alligator.

"Ssso . . . we like playing with Basil's trains, do we?"

Measle swallowed hard. He'd never been so frightened in his life. "I'm s-sorry, Mr. Tramplebone, s-sir," he managed to stammer.

"Sssorry?"

"I didn't mean for them to crash, r-really I didn't."

"Crash? There has been no crash, boy. Look for yoursssself."

Measle did as he was told. He swiveled around and stared at the train set. It was true. There was no sign of a crash. In fact, the section of track where the two trains *should* have been (lying, as Measle imagined they would be, in a tangled pile of wreckage) was empty. Measle looked in wonder, and he saw that the monster locomotive was back in its siding and the little green freight train was back at its starting point, right over there on the far side of the huge table. The humming sound of the electricity was gone, and all was quiet and peaceful and in its right and proper place.

"Mind you," said Basil, his voice a whisper, very close to Measle's ear, "mind you, there *would* have been a crash. A very nasssty crash, had I not arrived in the nick of time. And do you know how I arrived in the nick of time, Measle?"

"N-no, sir."

"Then I shall tell you. I arrived in the nick of time because, halfway to the bank, I realized that today is *Sssunday*. Sssunday, Measle. And you know what Sssunday means, don't you, Measle?"

"N-no, sir."

"Sssunday means that the banksss are *closed*, Measle. Including *our* bank, Measle. Ssso—it follows that we never had a call from the man at the bank thisss morning, doesn't it, Measle?"

"Y-yes, s-sir."

"It follows that you made the ssstory up, doesn't it, Measle?"

"Y-yes, s-sir."

"You lied to me, didn't you, Measle? You told me a falsssehood. And you tampered with the telephone, didn't you, Measle?"

"I'm really, r-really sorry, Mr. Tramplebone, sir."

Basil patted Measle gently on his shoulder, and Measle could feel the cold of Basil's fingers through the thin material of his shirt. "Of coursssse you're sssorry," whispered Basil. "And quite sssoon, you're going to be even sssorrier."

A bone-chilling coldness flooded through Measle's body, and at the same time he could feel beads of sweat oozing out on his face. He took a deep, shuddering breath. "What are you g-going to do?"

"Ah, there's the quessstion. What am I going to do? Well, Measle—I have always believed that the punishment should fit the crime. Do you believe that, Measle?"

"I s-suppose so, sir."

"You sssuppose ssso? Good. I sssuppose ssso, too. Very well. The punishment for playing with my train ssset—without my permission—is that you will play *in* my train ssset, with my *full* permission, for the ressst of your life."

What could he mean?

"P-play with your train set, sir?" stammered Measle.

"No, boy. You mussst try and lisssten when people talk to you. Not play *with* my train ssset. Play *in* my train ssset. Forever and ever and ever. Now, sssit perfectly ssstill and you won't get hurt."

And then Basil leaned very close to Measle, and he breathed softly into Measle's face.

Measle tried hard not to, but he screwed up his face as though he'd just eaten a lemon. Basil's breath was foul. It smelled of dead fish and old mattresses and the insides of ancient sneakers. Measle tried to lean away from the stench but Basil kept on breathing at him, until it seemed impossible to Measle that such a thin chest could contain so much air. Even when Measle felt sure that Basil couldn't possibly breathe out anymore without taking a breath *in*, Basil simply went on producing the soft, disgusting breeze and blowing it gently into Measle's face. Measle tried to hold his breath so he wouldn't have to smell it, but eventually he was forced to take a great gulp of air and, if anything, the smell was worse.

And Basil seemed to be getting bigger. The more he breathed out, the bigger Basil seemed to grow. Now he was towering over Measle, his head the size of a bus—but that was impossible, surely? A bus would never fit in the attic—and for a moment, Measle dragged his eyes away from Basil's staring goldfish eyes and looked about him.

Basil wasn't getting bigger. Measle was getting smaller.

Already, the stool on which he'd been sitting stretched away on either side of him, as if it wasn't a stool at all, but more like a broad table. And now his feet no longer dangled a few inches from the floor. Now the floor was a long, long way down and Measle appeared to be sitting on the edge of a high cliff, looking down at a drop that, if he fell, would certainly kill him.

Measle shuddered and scrambled back from the edge of the stool—and still Basil went on breathing over him and now the breeze was becoming a wind— and now it was a hurricane, which forced Measle to fall back, so that he was lying face upward on the flat wooden surface of the stool. He glanced to one side, trying to turn his face away from the dreadful smell, and he saw that the edge of the stool seemed to be far, far away.

And then the hurricane stopped. Measle turned his head and stared up at Basil in horror. Basil was vast, tall as a mountain—a mountain of black, topped by the stark whiteness of his face, so that he looked to Measle like the snowcapped peak of Mount Everest.

"There now," said Basil, his voice a distant boom. "We've cut you down to sssize, haven't we, Measle? Oh yesss. I should have done thisss years ago but we had to keep up appearanssses, didn't we? Oh yesss. But now—well, we don't really need you anymore, do we? You sssee, two weeksss ago, our bank appointed a new bank manager. Oh yesss. And our new bank manager, Mr. Griswold Grissstle, is one of usss—well, one of *me*, I should sssay—and a very, very friendly fellow indeed . . . at leassst to *me*. We had a deliciousss conversssation at the beginning of lassst week, Mr. Grissstle and I. And, well, the upshot of it all was that you were far too young to even *have* any money. Ssso all your lovely money is now in my control, Measle. It'sss mine, mine, *mine*. Ssso you sssee, dear boy—you are now sssuperfluousss to requirementsss."

Measle felt like crying but he didn't. Measle had finished with crying. He'd done a lot of it when he was younger but it hadn't changed a thing, so one day he'd simply stopped crying and hadn't cried since. Instead, he lay quite still, waiting to see what Basil would do next.

Basil said, "Ssstay there, Measle. Don't move a mussscle. Don't even blink, dear boy."

Measle thought that was an unnecessary thing to say. Where could he go? He was lying on a flat, wooden plain, surrounded on all sides by a long, distant drop to the floor far beneath him. He watched as Basil moved away to the other side of the attic. A moment later, he was back, looming huge over Measle. In his enormous right hand—it was the size of a house—he was holding something bright and silvery. The hand came slowly down toward Measle, and Measle saw that the bright, silvery object was a pair of tweezers—the same tweezers that Basil used when he was performing some particularly delicate task for his train set, like putting a new tree in place or rearranging the chips of coal in the coal yard. Now—to Measle—the tweezers looked gigantic; each leg of the instrument was as long as an oar and the points were coming steadily toward him—

"Lie quite ssstill, Measle," boomed Basil. "Thisss won't hurt if you lie quite ssstill."

Measle did as he was told. He'd learned never to argue with Basil. Besides, Basil never lied about anything. It was the only good thing you could say about him. Of course, the truth from Basil was never a *pleasant* truth—but it was always the truth. If Basil said that poisonous blue frogs would fall from the black cloud that hung permanently over the gloomy

33

house, you could be pretty sure that, before the day was out, the drains and the gutters would be full of very poisonous blue frogs. If Basil said it wouldn't hurt, then it wouldn't.

It *didn't* hurt, but it was unpleasant all the same. Measle watched the ends of the tweezers touch the front of his shirt—he felt the ends of the tweezers pinch together a wad of the material, then felt a pulling sensation as he was gently lifted up by his collar. Up and up he went, until the top of the stool was far beneath him, and the attic floor even farther. Measle kept very still. He knew that if he struggled, there was a good chance that his old shirt would split and that he'd drop away—and falling from this great height would certainly kill him. So he froze like a statue, his eyes wide open, praying that the collar of his shirt would hold.

Basil swung his enormous arm and Measle saw the great tabletop glide beneath him—the forest, the little wooden cabins, the railroad tracks, the sad, gray train yards with their sad, gray stations, and finally, the mound of coal chips in its own little fenced-in yard.

Measle felt himself going down. The ground seemed

to rush toward him, and he closed his eyes, expecting to feel a sickening crunch as his body hit—but, at the last moment, he suddenly slowed down, and he opened his eyes just wide enough to see that he was about to be deposited right in the middle of the coal heap.

Basil placed him carefully on the very top of the mound and then opened the tweezers. The strain on Measle's shirt collar was released.

"You always were sssuch a dirty boy," said Basil, his voice rumbling like a distant thunderstorm. "Now, you're even dirtier."

"Why are you doing this?" shouted Measle.

"What was that? A little sssqueak from a dirty little moussse? You'll have to ssspeak up, Measle—your voice is ssso tiny now, I can't hear you at all."

Measle struggled to his feet, glaring up at the black mountain that was Basil.

"Listen—I'm sorry I played with the train set!" he yelled, as loudly as he could. "I'll never do it again!"

"Ah—that'sss better. I can jussst about hear you now." Basil lowered his huge head, until his white face seemed to fill the whole sky. "Not play with my train ssset? Ever again? But Measle, my dear boy—you're welcome to it! Play *in* it as long as you like! Play in it forever! There's ssso much to do and ssso many things to sssee! Foresssts to eksssplore, houses to live in, people to talk to! Of courssse, I'm afraid they won't talk back because they can't—they're only made of plassstic—but at leassst they won't interrupt you when you tell them your life ssstory, will they? I do ssso hate it when people interrupt, don't you?"

He's mad, thought Measle. And then, because the thought was so strong, Measle raised his head and shouted, "You're mad!"

Basil smiled his terrible smile, revealing all six pointed yellow teeth. "Well, of courssse I am, Measle. And how very sssweet of you to sssay ssso. After that lovely compliment, I'm almossst tempted to let you go. But no—I think not. If I did, I wouldn't be mad, would I? And we can't have that now, can we? You sssee—being mad is sssuch enormousss *fun*! Enjoy yoursssself, young Measle. I'm going to leave you now, but I shall be back later to sssee how you're getting along."

Basil turned away—and then he paused and turned back again.

"One more thing, Measle—don't worry about food and drink. You will not ssstarve. If you look carefully, you'll find sssomething to eat. Sssomething very tasssty, I promissse. Bye-bye now."

Basil moved swiftly away toward the attic door, and Measle felt a sudden wind as a great mass of air rushed to fill the space that Basil had left behind him. He heard the attic door close, and a deep silence filled the room. Measle felt as alone as he'd ever felt in his life. Then he heard the attic door open again, and Basil's hissing whisper.

"Oh, Measle—jussst one more thing. A tiny word of warning. Ssstay under cover at night. It's not sssafe during the hours of darknesss—the long hours of darknesss. Not for a little moussselike creature sssuch as you. Hide at night, Measle. Hide well. Hide from the thing in the rafters, Measle."

There was a low *ssss-sss-sss* sound. For a moment, Measle couldn't imagine what it might be. Then he realized—it was Basil laughing.

The attic door closed again and the silence returned.

3

THE
CURE

Measle sat very still on the top of the coal pile for a long time. He hardly dared to breathe—because what Basil had said confirmed his worst fears. There *was* something up there in the rafters of the attic. Something dreadful. Something that would do him harm. Something that he must avoid at all costs.

Some *thing*.

After a while, Measle's paralyzed brain started to work again. Basil had said that the danger came during the long hours of darkness—which, of course, meant at nighttime. Basil never lied, which meant that Measle was safe during the day. It was still daylight. There, at the far end of the long room, was the distant window, with its grimy, broken panes of glass—and Measle could see that, while the sun wasn't shining outside (because it never shone over that grim, dark house), it was certainly out there somewhere, hidden behind the dismal black cloud but still providing enough light to the outside world to show that it existed.

Measle didn't have a watch, so he had no idea what the time was. He guessed it was about midafternoon. If Basil was telling the truth—and, in Measle's experience, he always did—Measle was safe from the *something* for several hours to come. He glanced quickly up toward the ceiling, just to check that there was no unspeakable horror there, poised to swoop down on him, its talons, or its beak, or its fangs, or its tentacles (or whatever terrifying features it possessed) stretched out to grab him. It was like looking up at a stormy sky. He was so tiny now and the ceiling was so very far away that the distant rafters were almost lost in the gloom. He peered upward, scanning the darkness. There was nothing up there—at least nothing he could see. Feeling far from safe but just safe enough to make a move off the coal heap, he inched himself down the side of the mound until he arrived on the ground below.

Through his fear, Measle couldn't help being amazed at the realism of his surroundings. The fence encircling the coal yard, like the coal heap itself with its actual lumps of coal, looked perfect in every detail. The wooden planks even had little knotholes in them, and the whole thing was covered with a thin layer of coal dust, just as it would be if the fence were full size. It was a drab and dirty place, and Measle decided that anywhere else on the huge table was probably going to be an improvement, so he headed for a gap in the fence and, a moment later, found himself in the heart of the rail yards.

There were two small freight engines standing next to each other. One had no wagons behind it. The other had three empty coal trucks linked to its tender. Both were filthy, covered with the kind of black grime you would expect to see on locomotives that were stationed near a coal yard. Measle gave them no more than a glance—he'd known that they would be there, having seen them only minutes before, when he was still full size. Instead, he picked his way across the railroad tracks, heading for the miniature town beyond them. The ground was lumpy and uneven, covered with the sort of rubbish you might expect in an old rail yard—bits of twisted metal, rotting wooden crates, rusting machine parts—and Measle had to walk carefully in order not to trip over anything.

At last he reached the edge of the rail yard. There was a building here, a long, low, brick building, with a slate roof. It was very realistic and Measle stopped for a moment to admire it. The bricks seemed old and several slates were missing from the roof. The glass in most of the windows was cracked or broken, and the whole building looked shabby and neglected. Measle picked his way toward it. There was a door hanging ajar on sagging hinges, and Measle cautiously poked his head inside and looked around. The building was empty. There was no furniture, no pictures, no rubbish, no nothing—simply the plain brick walls and a bare, rather new-looking wooden floor. Measle looked more closely at the floor. It was plywood, and it looked very much like the same kind of plywood that the huge table was made of. Measle knew what the table was made of because once when he and Basil were in the attic, the vibration of a passing train had caused a pine tree to fall off the edge of the table and down onto the floor. Basil had told Measle to pick it up. Measle had bent down and found the tree and, for a moment, had lingered there, looking up at the underside of the table. He saw that it was supported on eight rows of wooden trestles and that the tabletop itself was made of many sheets of smooth white birch plywood, which rested securely on the trestles.

The floor of the shabby building in which he now stood looked a lot like it was made from the same birch plywood. In that moment, Measle learned something: Basil only cared about what you could see. If it was visible from above, everything about the train set was correct, down to the smallest detail. If it *wasn't* visible from above, Basil didn't care about it. Measle tucked this bit of information away in his brain and walked quickly through the empty building to another door on the far side of the bare room. He pushed it open and found himself—as he knew he would—in a street of small, sooty houses.

At the far end of the street—which Measle knew

was quite near the edge of the great table—stood a pair of plastic figures. Measle remembered them; one was the man in the blue coat and the yellow helmet, sitting on the side of the pit, holding the electrical cables. The other figure, directly behind him, was the man with the bucket of water. Measle decided to take a closer look, so he walked quickly down the street toward them. As he got nearer, he noticed that there was a considerable difference between the two plastic figures. At close range, the man with the bucket of water was quite crudely modeled. His paintwork was rough and the seam where his two halves had been joined together in the factory was plain to see, running down the middle of his face and down his chest.

The man with the yellow helmet was something else entirely. He, too, was obviously made of plastic, but his hair and clothes—and even the lines of age on his face, and the graying hair poking out from under the yellow helmet—looked amazingly realistic. There was no seam running down his body either. Measle wondered if perhaps Basil hadn't bought him from one of his model railway catalogs but had actually made him himself. If so—well, it was a brilliant piece of craftsmanship. There was even a battered steel toolbox by the man's side——something Measle had never noticed before.

Beyond the two figures was the edge of the table, and near the edge, there was a small scattering of yellow objects and a broad puddle of pink liquid. For a moment, Measle couldn't imagine what they could be. Then he realized what they were: glazed doughnut crumbs and spilled pink lemonade, left there by Basil after one of his binges.

Measle suddenly felt hungry. His meager lunch seemed a long time ago, and it hadn't been much to speak of anyway. He'd always longed for a taste of Basil's glazed doughnuts and a sip of Basil's pink lemonade, and now, at last, he could eat and drink his fill of them. Perhaps, he thought, there was something to be said for being half an inch tall. Back when he was full size, what lay before him would have been nothing but a few crumbs and a single drop but now, in light of his miniature state, it was a feast that could last him several days. Obviously, that was what Basil had meant when he'd said that Measle would find plenty to eat and drink.

Well, he'd found it. Measle moved past the still,

silent figures of the two men, and when he reached the scattered doughnut crumbs, he bent down and picked up the biggest crumb and sniffed it. Yes, it was certainly doughnut. He opened his mouth—

"Nurrr."

The sound, very quiet and muffled, had come from behind him. Measle turned quickly. Apart from the two plastic men, the street was empty. Measle shook his head. He must have imagined it. He opened his mouth again—

"Nurrr!"

This time, Measle knew he hadn't imagined it. The sound came from close by—right where the figures of the men were placed. Was it possible that one of them was trying to say something to him? Measle stared hard at the figures and slowly raised the doughnut crumb to his mouth.

"Nurrr! Nurrr! Nurrr!"

It was the man with the yellow helmet. His mouth had moved—at least, one small corner of it. It had opened just wide enough for the sound to come out. There was no question about it: the voice had come from the plastic man and he was trying to say something.

Measle took a couple of careful steps toward the figure and then stopped. There was something creepy about all this, and Measle was scared.

"Wh-what did you say?" he stammered.

The corner of the mouth opened again. "Own eat."

"What?"

"Own eat onut. Own rink renonade."

Measle frowned. It sounded as if the man was trying to say "Don't eat doughnut—don't drink lemonade."

"You don't want me to eat this?" said Measle, holding up the doughnut crumb.

"Ri. Own eat. Own rink. Nedder, nedder, nedder."

"Why not?"

"End uck ike ee."

That one took a bit of thinking about. A moment later, Measle got it. "End up like you?"

"Ri."

Measle stared at the model. It was very strange being told not to do something by a plastic man. In fact, it was so strange that Measle forgot his fear and took two steps closer. He peered up at the man's face. There was no question about it—while amazingly realistic, he was still made entirely of plastic except, perhaps, for that small corner of his mouth. The rest of his face was smooth and shiny. The eyes stared blankly off into the distance, but the corner of the mouth looked a little different. There seemed to be something human about it, something alive.

"How can you talk? You're a plastic model, aren't you?"

"Ostly. Just a lil it left now."

"You mean—you're *alive*?"

"Not for uch longer. Soon I'll ee all lastic."

"Soon you'll be all plastic?"

"Yesh."

"But—how? Why?"

"De onuts. De lenonade. *Oison*."

"The doughnuts and the lemonade are poison?"

"Ri. They turn oo into lastic."

Measle looked about him. "But there's nothing else to eat. I'll starve to death."

"Etter an eing lastic."

Measle felt all hope draining from him. He knew he could probably last a few days but, eventually, he would become so weak for want of food and water that he'd no longer be able to walk, let alone search for food that

47

wasn't there. He sank slowly to his knees and, as he did so, he felt a pressure against his thigh from something in his pocket. He reached in and his fingers touched paper. Of course! It was the bag of carrots he'd taken from the refrigerator earlier that day. Measle pulled the bag out of his pocket and looked inside. He counted the carrots—twelve old, wrinkled things, some still crusted with the soil they'd grown in. If he was careful, he could make them last maybe six days—but after that?

He reached in and took out the cleanest.

"Ossat oo got ere?"

"Just an old carrot."

"*A arrot?*" There was a combination of amazement and longing in the man's voice as if, at first, he couldn't believe what he'd heard and, then, if he *had* heard it right, he couldn't believe that something so wonderful could be so close to him.

Measle looked up at him and said, "You want some?"

There was a pause, then the man, in a tone of great sadness, said, "On't ink I can chew it. Outh on't erk."

"Your mouth doesn't work?"

"Ri."

"I could cut it up for you—that is, if you can still swallow?"

There was another pause, and then Measle heard a gulping sound.

"I can do at," said the man, suddenly sounding much happier.

"Good," said Measle. Then he said, "Um—trouble is, I haven't got a knife."

"Ook in de ool ox."

Look in the toolbox. Measle squatted down and opened the battered toolbox. Inside, there was a lift-out tray with lots of small compartments. The compartments held electrical connectors and screws and staples and nails—but nothing to cut a carrot with.

"Unnerneath," said the plastic man.

Measle lifted out the tray. Down in the bottom of the box was a jumbled pile of tools—hammers and saws and screwdrivers and drills and chisels—and right at the very bottom was a folding penknife. It had a handle made from deer horn and a long, curved blade. It was the sort of knife Measle had always wanted, but Basil would never have let him have one. Basil wouldn't let him have anything of his own, apart from his few dirty old clothes. Measle stared at the knife for a moment, a grin spreading over his face.

"Oo want at?" said the man.

Measle felt himself going red. He nodded.

"Iss oors."

Measle went even redder. He hadn't had a present in years, not since his parents were alive. Measle didn't remember when his birthday was and, even if he *had* known, he was sure that Basil would've ignored it. And as for Christmas . . .

"Thank you very much."

"Oo're elcome."

Measle wiped a patch of roadway in front of him with the end of his sleeve, until it was as clean as he could get it. Then he put the carrot down on the spot, opened the penknife and began to chop the carrot into small pieces.

"When was the last time you had something to eat?" he asked.

"On't know—aybe six years. Onuts and lenonade."

"Six *years*? You must be starving!"

"En oo're lastic, oo don't tarve. Jus get erry, erry ungry."

"Well, here you are."

Measle scooped up the chopped carrot and carefully, piece by piece, pushed the little cubes into the corner of the man's mouth.

"Good. Erry good," said the man between swallows. "Etter an onuts and lenonade."

Measle went on feeding the man until all the chopped carrot was gone.

"Ank oo," said the man.

Then Measle saw a very odd thing. The man began to move the side of his mouth in and out, in and out—and then, suddenly, he was moving his whole mouth. Now the rest of it no longer looked as if it was made of hard plastic—now it was a truly human mouth. The man opened it and said, quite clearly and without any of the muffled sound, "Thank you very much, Measle."

And then the man's eyebrows shot up to the top of his forehead, as if he was as surprised at this new sound as Measle was—and Measle was very surprised indeed.

Measle said, "You can talk properly now!"

"Looks like I can," said the man, and he opened his mouth wide, stretching his jaw muscles and wiggling his tongue. "Well, who'd have thought it? Must be the effects of the carrot."

"The *carrot* did it?"

"Can't think what else," said the man, suddenly dropping the electric cables, raising his right arm and touching his face with his hand.

"You can move!" shouted Measle.

"So I can!"

The man stared at his hand. He flexed the fingers, watching them bend and straighten. Then he lifted his left arm and scratched his ear. "I've been dying to do that for six years," he said. "Now, let's see about the legs, shall we?"

Slowly the man pulled himself to his feet. Then he leaned forward and lifted one foot and took a step. He swayed and grabbed Measle's shoulder. "A bit wobbly, but I think I'm getting better."

Measle stared at him in wonder. There, standing by his side and leaning heavily on his shoulder, was a living, breathing human man, with all trace of plastic gone from his appearance.

"I can't believe a carrot could do that," he said. "It doesn't make any sense."

The man looked down at him and smiled. "It makes the same kind of sense as doughnuts and lemonade

52

turning you into plastic, don't you think? It makes as much sense as this whole situation. I mean, look at us! We're half an inch tall, prisoners on top of a table, stuck in a model railway set. If *that* makes any sense to you, Measle, then you must be pretty peculiar."

"I suppose I am——a bit," said Measle.

"No, you're not," said the man, patting Measle on the shoulder. "You're a hero, that's what you are. Look, you brought me back to life, didn't you? That makes you a hero, Measle."

"How do you know my name?"

The man looked gloomy. "Well, that's part of the cruelty of it all. I may have been plastic, but that doesn't mean I couldn't still hear and see. I've watched you, watching us, all the time I've been here. Couldn't move, could hardly speak, and hungry as a horse——but I could see and hear everything that goes on. That's how I know your name——listening to Basil Tramplebone. 'Pick that up, Measle.' 'Put that down, Measle.' 'Sit still, Measle.' And I'll tell you something else, young Measle——I don't think that Basil is quite human."

"I'm absolutely sure he's not," said Measle.

"What do you think he is?"

"I don't know," said Measle. "And I don't think I want to know."

The man nodded thoughtfully. Then he took a deep breath and said, "Come on. Let's head for the center of town. There may be a few others we can work the carrot magic on. Know the way, do you?"

Measle nodded. The two of them set off, walking quickly back along the street toward a crossroads in the distance. Measle remembered that by turning right they would come to the side street that led to the main part of the town. As they walked, he asked the man his name.

"Frank," said the man. "Frank Hunter."

"How did you get here?"

"Same way you did. It seems to happen to anybody who makes Mr. Tramplebone angry. See, I'm an electrician. I put in the wiring for the train set. It was all built and ready to go, except for the electrics. When I'd finished, he seemed happy with what I'd done. Then I gave him the bill. All of a sudden, he wasn't happy at all. In fact, he refused to pay it. We got into an argument. Next thing I know, I'm half an inch tall, wandering about in his train set. I ate the crumbs of doughnuts and drank the drops of lemonade—all the time trying to keep out of his sight—and slowly, I got stiffer and stiffer and stiffer, until I couldn't move at all. Of course, there's something special about Basil's dough-nuts and his lemonade. I mean to say, we all know that stuff's bad for you—but not *that* bad."

"But what about how I found you? I mean, you with the electric wires—and the man with the bucket of water? What was all that about?"

Frank shook his head. "I dunno," he said. "Basil likes to change things around, and once you're unable to move, he can put you into any position he likes. A few weeks ago, I was up a telegraph pole. Before that, he had me changing a lightbulb in one of the streetlamps. Then Basil started rearranging stuff again, and there I am being menaced by a man with a bucket of water. Of course, I was in no danger, but all the same—it was a bit creepy, knowing he was behind me like that."

Measle stopped so suddenly that Frank walked on a couple of steps before he realized that Measle was no longer by his side. Then he, too, stopped and looked back at Measle.

"What is it?"

"I know which ones to rescue," said Measle.

"You do? Who?"

"They're the ones Basil put into weird situations. There's a bunch of them and they're all in some sort of danger. Well, *pretend* danger. Just like you. There's one in the town square, there's a couple in the forest—one near the second station—"

Frank grinned. "Well, come on then," he said. "What are we waiting for? Town square first, I think. It's nearest, isn't it?"

They walked quickly to the town square. There was the suggestion of a park here, with a worn patch of grass (in reality, it was painted sandpaper) and a few sad-looking trees made from papier-mâché. In the middle of the square was a statue, set high on a stone base.

The statue was of a man and a woman. The woman was kneeling by the man's side and her arm was thrown across her face, as if she couldn't bear to see what was in front of her. The man stood straight and tall beside her, his right hand extended forward, his palm facing outward, as if he was trying to stop something that was approaching. At the bottom of the statue, carved into the stone base, were some words. Measle had often tried to read them when he was watching Basil play with his trains, but the writing was too small and too far away from where he used to sit, so he'd never known what they said. Now, half an inch tall and standing in the shadow of the statue, he could read them quite clearly.

IN MEMORIAM.
VENI, VIDI, VICI.
REQUIESCANT IN PACE.
HA HA HA.

"What does it mean?" asked Measle, looking up at the statue.

"Well," said Frank, slowly, "I think it's Latin. I know the first one. It means 'In memory.' I don't know what the one underneath it means. The next means 'Rest in peace.'"

"And the 'HA HA HA'?"

Frank looked suddenly angry. "I think that's Basil laughing," he said. "Come on—let's rescue that woman from the plastic tiger, shall we?"

They approached the steps of the town hall, where

the figures of the crouching woman and the menacing Bengal tiger were positioned. As they passed the tiger, Measle could clearly see that it was just a shop-bought model, the most obvious evidence being the rough paintwork on its body and face and the raised seam that ran down the length of its back. The woman looked much more lifelike. She was dressed in a smart suit—a gray skirt with a matching gray jacket and a white blouse. Her shoes were black, with high heels, and there was an expensive-looking leather handbag beside her. She was leaning forward, her elbows on the ground, her head buried in her hands. Frank knelt down in front of her.

"Miss? Can you talk, miss?"

"Yes," said the woman, her voice very soft and low, but quite distinct. "But I'm not a 'miss.' I'm a lady."

"Of course you are, miss," said Frank kindly.

"No, you don't understand," muttered the woman. "My name is Lady Grant, you see. Lady Mary Grant."

"Oh," said Frank. He turned his head and winked at Measle. "So sorry, Lady Grant."

"Oh, please help me!" said Lady Grant. "I've been staring at the ground for such a long time—and I can't move at all. Oh, please—whoever you are—can you do something?"

Frank grinned at Measle. "Let me have a carrot, Measle," he said. "No, on second thought, just a little bit of a carrot. It may be enough—she's not as bad as I was—and we've got to make them last."

Measle took the smallest carrot out of the paper bag, opened the penknife and cut a small chip off it. He handed it to Frank, who gently pushed the chip into the woman's mouth.

"Can you bite that?" he asked.

"Yes, I think so. What is it? And I do hope you washed your hands? Oh—it's a carrot. Why are you giving me a carrot?"

"You'll see," said Frank.

There was a crunching sound as the woman began to chew. She said, "It's all gritty. And I don't terribly care for raw carrots—" And then she stopped talking because, slowly, her head was beginning to raise itself and, a moment later, she was sitting upright. "Oh, how marvelous," she said in a grand voice, smiling in aston-ishment. "This is wonderful. I can't thank you enough." She looked closely at Frank, and her eyes widened. "I know you," she said. "You're the man near the coal yard, aren't you? When I could still move, I saw you there."

Frank said, "The name's Hunter, Lady Grant. Frank Hunter." He touched Measle on the shoulder and gently pushed him forward. "And this is your rescuer."

She stared at Measle, her eyes widening with growing horror. "Oh my goodness. You're the boy, aren't you? The giant boy! You're in league with that revolting Tramplebone creature!"

"Not in league at all, Lady Grant," said Frank. "And not a giant anymore, as you may have noticed. Basil's done to him what he did to all of us. He just rescued you. This is Measle."

"Yes, *Measle*," cried Lady Grant. "That's your unfortunate name, isn't it? So you're not Tramplebone's friend then?"

Measle shook his head. "I hate him," he muttered.

Lady Grant clasped her hands under her chin. "Oh, I'm so glad. I mean, I know one isn't supposed to hate anybody, but I'm afraid I've had to make an exception in Tramplebone's case. Well, Measle—what an odd name—I don't know how to thank you."

Measle's face went pink. Nobody had ever said "thank

you" to him in his entire life, and now he'd been thanked twice in the last few minutes and he really wasn't used to it. He opened his mouth to say something, but Lady Grant raised her hand. "No, no," she said. "No need to say anything. Now, I wonder what I could do to repay you—once we're out of this revolting situation, I mean." She gazed at him, her eyes slowly taking him in. She sniffed and then wrinkled her nose. "Well, perhaps a visit to a bathroom to start with—and then, my dear, well something will simply *have* to be done about it!"

"Done about what?" said Measle.

"Dear boy—your hair! I've never seen anything quite like it in my entire life. It looks as though some-body's been chopping at it with a kitchen knife!"

"How did you know?" said Measle.

Lady Grant blinked several times. "You mean—I was *right*? Good heavens! Well, never mind—my personal hairdresser will know what to do with it."

"So . . . what happened to you, Lady Grant?" asked Frank.

"Well, I'm a borough councillor, you see. At least, I *was* a borough councillor. From the town hall. We had sent several letters to Mr. Tramplebone about the state of his house, but he never replied to any of them. I really don't care to be ignored, so I came in person—at some inconvenience—to tell Mr. Tramplebone that his house was in a terrible state of repair and that he was to do something about it. His drains, too. They were blocking the main sewer up with some sort of revolting green globs—"

Measle nodded. "That's our bathwater," he said. Measle began to wonder if perhaps *revolting* was her favorite word.

Lady Grant stared at Measle for a moment, as if she couldn't quite believe he'd said that. Then she blinked and started to speak again. "Anyway, I told him that he had to make certain repairs within the next six months, or steps would be taken against him. He just looked at me with those frightful eyes and then he started breathing on me—and his breath was *revolting*—and the next thing I know, I'm half an inch tall, wandering about in this ridiculous little fake town."

"See what I mean?" said Frank to Measle. "Anybody who makes Basil angry gets it and gets it good."

"He's a *revolting* creature, that's all I know," said Lady Grant.

4

THE
VICTIMS

During the next hour and a half, Measle, Frank and Lady Grant brought the remaining four people back to life.

The first was nearby, in a long street that led toward the forest. Measle led them to the spot where he'd seen the tableau of the little round bald man being chased by the angry mob. Ignoring the plastic pursuers and their placards, they went directly to the little man and fed him some chips of carrot, and moments later he dropped his heavy suitcase and sat down in the middle of the road. He shook his head and wiped his shiny forehead with the sleeve of his coat.

"Phew," he gasped. "You only just got here in time. They nearly had me."

Measle said, "No, they couldn't have. Honestly. They're only plastic, you see."

The little man looked up at him and grinned. He put his right forefinger alongside his nose and tapped it knowingly. "I know that, kid. That was a little joke, you see. I make lots of little jokes. You'll get used to it."

He pulled himself to his feet, breathing heavily. "Grateful thanks all around. The name's Durham. William O. Durham. Don't ask what the O stands for—'cause it doesn't stand for anything, see? 'O'—geddit? Zero, in other words. Well, you've got to laugh, haven't you?"

"I don't see why," sniffed Lady Grant.

William turned out to be a traveling salesman who had tried to sell a set of expensive encyclopedias to Basil a year and a half ago. He'd stood on the doorstep and done his salesman chat, and when Basil had tried to close the door, William had stuck his foot in the gap. A moment later, Basil's bony hand had reached out and dragged

William into the house by his shirt front and . . .

"What a nasty piece of work," William said. "Even nastier than my boss—and that's saying something. At least my boss doesn't have bad breath. Dear, oh dear. We all got a good whiff of Basil's, though, didn't we? Phew, what a stink, eh? Now then—where are my samples?"

He pulled his suitcase onto his knees and snapped open the catches. He lifted the lid and nodded with satisfaction. The case was packed tight with encyclopedias.

"All here still. Well, there's a turnup for the books." When nobody laughed, he said, "*Books*. Turnup for the *books*. 'Cause I sell them, see? Another little joke. I've got millions of them."

Lady Grant made a face. "Well, perhaps we don't need to hear them all at once, Mr. Durham."

Frank broke the awkward silence that followed.

"Come on then, Measle," he said cheerfully. "Let's go get the rest of them."

Next to be rescued was the little girl. Frank pushed the three black plastic bears away from the base of the pine tree in order to give the humans room to move. They decided that the best thing to do was for Measle to climb up to the girl with a few carrot chips and feed them to her while she was still up in the tree. Frank gave Measle the harness that he'd used when mending power lines at the top of telegraph poles and showed him how to fasten it around the girl so that she wouldn't fall.

"And you be careful up there, Measle," he said. "We don't want to lose you."

The pine tree was easy to climb, with lots of branches all the way up. Measle quickly reached the girl. Her arms were wrapped tightly around the trunk and her cheek was pressed hard against the rough bark. Her eyes were shut tight, and when Measle touched her on the shoulder, she gasped.

"It's all right," he whispered. "I'm just going to tie this around you. It'll stop you from falling, you see. There— now swallow this. Don't worry, you'll be all right."

Measle fed her a small piece of carrot, and a few moments later she let go of the trunk, threw her arms around his neck and burst into tears.

"Ooh—thank you, thank you, thank you!" she sobbed.

Measle went even pinker than when Lady Grant had thanked him. The little girl's tears were soaking into his old shirt.

"Can you climb down?" he asked, hoping that this was something that Brownies could do at least as well as they could cry. The little girl sniffed and nodded, so Measle carefully untied Frank's harness and the girl scrambled down the tree in a way that suggested that tree climbing was a Brownie speciality.

Everybody clustered around her, and soon she stopped crying and was able to tell her story. Her name was Kitty Webb and she had come to the house—much against her better judgment—to try to sell some Brownie cookies to Basil. When Basil had opened the door, Kitty had taken one look at him and then—sensibly—had tried to run away. But Basil had caught her with one of his bony yellow hands and the rest was history.

Lady Grant took a tissue from her handbag and wiped away the traces of Kitty's tears. "What a charming uniform," she cooed. "So smart—quite like my designer suit. And so many badges. What a clever girl you must be."

"Who's next, Measle?" asked Frank.

"Um—well, there's the man in the forest. Near the lake."

"We're right behind you."

Measle led them to the clearing. The walk took several minutes, and halfway there, Lady Grant, trailing in the rear, moaned and said, "Is it very much farther? It's just that these shoes are not designed for walking in the woods, you see."

William O. Durham looked back at her and laughed shortly. "Ho! You should try carrying a suitcase of encyclopedias around, lady. Weigh half a ton, these do. Very heavy stuff, is knowledge. That's why clever people have such big heads, you see. It's all that extra weight they're lugging about."

Soon they reached the clearing. They stood in a circle, staring at the enormous black man sitting on the tree stump. The man was huge, almost an inch tall (which made him, Measle calculated, about six feet six inches in real life). His plastic chest bulged with plastic muscles; his plastic arms were as thick as trees. His mouth was a line of plastic with no opening between the lips. There didn't seem to be any part of him that wasn't hard, unyielding plastic. When they spoke to him, there was no response.

William said, "Do you think he's alive?"

"There's one way to find out," said Frank. He reached into his toolbox and brought out a little round mirror on the end of a metal stick. "I use it to see around difficult corners," he explained. Frank put the mirror close to the plastic man's nose. Then he took it away and examined it closely. "Look at this," he said.

They all clustered around the little mirror. It was clouded, as if someone had breathed on it. "His lungs are working," said Frank. "Question is, how do we get the carrot inside him?"

William said, "Wait a minute. Let me have a look at my books." He sat down on a nearby stump and opened his suitcase. He pulled out an encyclopedia, flipping quickly through the pages. Then he rose and returned to the group.

"There!" he said, pointing to a page.

It was a section on human anatomy, and the picture that William was pointing at was an illustration of the inside of a man's head. It showed the brain, the nose, the mouth and the throat—and how they were all connected. "Look," said William, tracing his finger over the picture. "See how the nasal passages join up to the back of the throat? This chap is still breathing. I reckon if we can cut the carrot very small—and if the chap can sniff really hard—we might be able to get enough into him."

"It's going to be frightfully uncomfortable for him," said Lady Grant.

"But better than ending up solid plastic," said Frank. "I know—Measle got to me just in time. Another few months . . ." His voice trailed away.

William closed his encyclopedia with a bang. "First, we're going to have to see if the chap can sniff that hard." He moved close to the plastic figure and shouted into its face. "Hey, old chap! Can you sniff really *hard*?"

They all heard it: the sound of a strong intake of breath through the plastic nostrils.

"Good!" said William. He turned to Measle. "I think we're going to need a lot of carrot for this chap—and chopped very small. As small as you can get it."

Measle set to work. Quite soon, he had a small heap of finely chopped carrot on the ground in front of him. William took one tiny piece and put it on the palm of his hand. Then he lifted his hand close to the man's nose. "Right, mate," he said. "This might be a bit uncomfortable—and you've got to try and stop it going into your lungs—but it's worked for the rest of us, so it's going to work for you, too. Go on, now— sniff as hard as you can."

Sniff.

The tiny piece of carrot disappeared into the plastic man's nose. A moment later, there was a coughing, choking sound—then silence.

"You okay?" said William. "Sniff twice if you are."

Sniff. Sniff.

"Did it go down all right? Down into the old tum- tum?"

Sniff. Sniff.

"I guess it did," said William. "Ready to try again?"

Sniff. Sniff.

It took half an hour to get twenty tiny pieces of carrot into the man, and most of them were accompa- nied by the coughing, choking noises. Measle began to feel very sorry for the man—and then he saw a sudden twitching at the corner of the man's mouth. The twitching turned into a small opening in the plastic, which suddenly wasn't plastic anymore. Now it was human flesh—

William was about to put another carrot chip into the man's nose. "Wait!" shouted Measle. "Look—look at his mouth!"

After that, it was easy. It still took a long time, and the pieces of carrot went in very slowly, but there was no more coughing or choking, and more and more of the man's face became human, with human skin and muscles over human bone. Quite soon he was talking, in a slurred and slushy voice.

"Boy, am I glad *that's* over. You ever take food up your nose? Let me tell you—you don't want to do it. But thanks. Thanks a million. Name's Kip. Kip Lovell."

"You've been here a very long time," said Frank.

Kip nodded. "I've been here since the beginning. I'm a carpenter; I built this table for Mr. Tramplebone. When I'd finished, he complained that the edges were too rough, so I was up here one day, sanding them down, when suddenly he started breathing into my face—"

"So revolting," said Lady Grant.

"Next thing I know, I'm down to the size of a nail,

stuck on this tabletop. Tramplebone made me help him build the model. At first, he fed me properly—little bits of meat and vegetables, a drop of water now and then. But once the place was pretty much finished, he started leaving his doughnut crumbs and his lemonade, and, well, that was the end of me. I watched you all arrive. I watched you, young Measle—and I wondered how long it would be before you joined us. Now I know."

Kip picked up his carpenter's bag, his chain saw and the red fuel tank and rose to his feet, towering head and shoulders over the rest of them. He turned and surveyed the three plastic lumberjacks behind him. "That Basil—he's got some sick imagination."

"He's got a sick *everything*," said William, packing away his encyclopedia. "I mean to say—having breath so horrible that it shrinks a chap like me down to the size of a pushpin. Dear, oh dear. There must be something seriously wrong with his stomach. Stands to reason, doesn't it?"

"I don't think reason comes into it," said Frank. "I think, with Basil Tramplebone, you've got to throw reason out of the window."

William shook his shiny round head. "I'd like to throw *him* out of the window. But there's got to be a scientific explanation for all this, hasn't there?"

Lady Grant snorted. "Well, if there is one, I'd like to hear it."

There was a short silence while everybody thought about this. Then William opened his mouth—but Frank got in before he could say anything.

"Is there anybody else, Measle?" he asked.

"Um—there's the old lady."

Frank nodded. "I remember her. Where is she?"

Measle pointed back toward the town. "She's in a siding at the second station, the one on the branch line."

Kip stepped into their midst. He looked up at the distant attic window. "We'd better hurry," he said. "There's not much daylight left."

When they reached the old lady, they hurriedly pushed aside the plastic figures that were clustered around her. Kip took a sharp utility knife from his tool bag and cut the ropes that bound her to the railway tracks. Her mouth was still working normally, and she was able to gasp out her thanks as they lifted her clear of the rails and laid her gently on a bench on the station platform. Measle fed her some chips of carrot—he noticed that they'd used up nearly half his supply—and a few moments later the old lady was able to sit up.

Her name was Prudence Peyser, and she was much older than the rest of the adults, with a mop of untidy gray hair and lots of wrinkles on her face. She was dressed in an old green nylon jacket and a tweed skirt. A pair of sensible-looking shoes was on her feet, and thick woolen stockings encased her legs. When they brought her back to life and asked her who she was, she told them her name and then she said, "I'm a wrath-monkologist."

"A what?" said Measle.

Prudence looked embarrassed. She said, "A wrath-monkologist. It's a silly name, I know. And a lot of people think what I do is pretty silly. I go around studying Wrathmonks. Most people don't know what they are—and, even if they do, they don't believe in them."

William said, "I never heard of them. What are Wrathmonks?"

Prudence said, "Well, you've all heard of sorcerers, I suppose?"

Everybody nodded their heads. William said, "*Heard* of 'em, yes. But if they're not in the encyclopedia— and they're not because I've read 'em all, cover to cover—well, as far as I'm concerned, they don't exist."

"Well," said Prudence, "that's because the people who write encyclopedias don't *believe* they exist. One can't really blame them, I suppose. Not in this day and age. But perhaps you'll change your minds when you hear this. Now, *Sorcerers* is the general word for all three levels of wizardry—"

"Oh, there's *three* levels, are there?" said William in a sneery voice.

Prudence sighed. "Yes, Mr. Durham, there are. I know none of this is in your encyclopedia, but then neither are *you*—and yet *you* exist, don't you?"

William opened his mouth to say something and then thought better of it. Instead, he simply said, "Humph," and stared at the ground. Measle grinned inwardly. He was beginning to like this old lady.

Prudence went on. "Now, as you probably know from the fairy stories, Wizards are supposed to be reasonably good and kind, and use their powers only to improve things. Merlin was the best example, I suppose—if he ever existed, of course. There are still quite a few Wizards around, but most of them live very quietly nowadays. They like collecting stamps and listening to classical music and mending old clocks. In fact, if you ever come across an old gentleman—or an old lady, come to that; Sorcerers can be male or female—if you ever come across somebody who likes doing all three of those things, then you can be pretty sure he or she is a Wizard, and there's nothing much to fear from a Wizard. Next, we have Warlocks. Warlocks are Wizards who have a dark side to them—they mostly use their powers for good but sometimes they don't. Quite a lot of Warlocks become lawyers, and we know about *them*, don't we? Others go into politics. You can always tell a politician who's really a Warlock—they try to stop anything new happening and they don't much care for young people. They dress in very expensive clothes, drive very expensive cars and drink a lot of very expensive wine. You don't have to fear them—just be a bit careful when you're around one. Last, you have the Wrathmonks. Wrathmonks are another thing altogether. You should be very, very frightened when you're anywhere *near* a Wrathmonk.

You see, Wrathmonks are Warlocks who have gone mad. Wizards never go mad but Warlocks do occasionally (it's got something to do with all the stress in their lives, I think), and when they do, they become Wrathmonks. Thank heavens it's quite a rare event, because there's nothing you can do with a Wrathmonk. All the dark side comes pouring out of them, and they're completely out of control. Wizards and Warlocks hate them and are afraid of them, probably because a Wrathmonk's insanity is what makes him so powerful. They don't think before they act, which makes their power very pure. And pure power is unstoppable."

"And—Basil is one of them?" said Frank.

"As far as I can determine, yes," said Prudence.

"Whatever he is," said Lady Grant, "he's a revolting creature."

"I don't know about all this," said William dubiously. "Wizards and Warlocks and Wrathmonks. What about Witches, then?"

Prudence shook her gray curls. "Witches are something else entirely, Mr. Durham. They have no magical powers at all. Witchcraft is all to do with the sacred meaning of nature and is not to be confused with sorcery in any way."

William sniffed. "I don't know. Dear, oh dear. I mean, it's all a bit farfetched, isn't it?"

Frank shifted his yellow helmet off his forehead and scratched his head. "I think if Miss Prudence says there are such things, we ought to believe in them. After all, the proof's right here."

"I don't know," said William, shaking his head. "I mean—it's not *scientific*, is it? Not like my books."

"Your books are all very well," said Frank. "All very well in the *real* world. But you're not in the real world now, are you? Just look around you!"

William gazed gloomily at his surroundings. "Right. You've got a point there. I suppose it's just possible these Wrathmonks do exist."

"Of course there are Wrathmonks!" cried Kitty. Everybody turned in surprise and stared at her. She'd been very quiet all this time, staying close to Measle all the way back from the forest and not saying a word to anyone. Now she blushed a deep red and stared hard at the ground. "I believe in them," she said, so quietly that her words could hardly be heard.

Kip nodded. "So do I. It's crazy not to, seeing as we're all victims of one."

Prudence looked relieved. "I'm glad you agree. You see, I've been studying Basil Tramplebone for some time. Of course, I could never get near him, but I'd been watching the house for six months. It was the rain cloud that gave him away. Wrathmonks always have rain clouds hanging over them. It's part of that dark side I was telling you about. Anyway, one day, I got careless and Basil caught me watching the house, and quick as a flash, here I am."

"Is Basil a very *powerful* writh—wroth—um—webfink?" asked Measle, nervously.

"*Wrathmonk,*" said Prudence. "They're all very powerful. Thank goodness, there aren't that many of them. Basil's one of the meanest and nastiest I've ever seen."

"Is there anything that can be done—against them, I mean?" asked Frank.

Prudence shook her head. "Not really. It's generally believed by wrathmonkologists that a Wrathmonk's spell is actually stronger than he is—which means that, if there were some way of turning the Wrathmonk's spell back at him, he wouldn't be able to resist it. But as far as I know, nobody's ever succeeded in doing that, so it's only a theory."

There was a grim silence, while everybody thought about this. Then Prudence said, "By the way, has anybody seen my little dog? He's black and white and a bit of a mongrel, I'm afraid—"

"Is the dog yours?" said Measle, who had always liked the fact that there was a model dog in the train set. "I know where he is."

"Do you think," said Prudence eagerly, "do you think you could spare a very small piece of carrot for him? I'm very fond of Tinker, you see."

They found Tinker by the streetlamp. He was a scruffy little black-and-white wirehaired terrier, with a stubby tail that stood up straight from his back like a short, furry finger. Feeding him pieces of carrot was difficult. Tinker kept trying to spit them out, but they kept on pushing the pieces into his mouth until he was forced to swallow—and a moment later he was up on his feet, bounding around them all and barking like crazy.

"That's how Basil caught us," said Prudence. "Tinker couldn't help barking whenever he saw Basil. I think he really hates Wrathmonks more than I do."

Lady Grant's shoulders slumped and she stared at the ground in despair.

"Now, now," said Prudence, briskly. "Let's not give up hope. Look at us! We're alive again, thanks to Measle."

"But how are we going to *stay* alive?" moaned Lady Grant. "We all know we can't get off the table—it's far too high off the ground. Which means we're stuck here for good. We can't exist on Measle's carrots, can we? I don't suppose there are that many left."

Measle looked in the paper bag. There were five whole carrots still there, along with several small pieces left over from the chopping process. "You're right," he said. "There aren't many left."

"Ooohh," wailed Lady Grant. "We're all going to starve to death!"

"No," said Measle, slowly. "No, I don't think so."

"Of course we are!" Lady Grant cried. "We'll be through those carrots in a few days! And then what?"

"Well . . . ," said Measle shyly, because he wasn't at all sure these grown-ups would think that anything he had to say would be worth much. "Well—surely if a little piece of carrot can bring you back to life, then couldn't we eat the doughnut crumbs and drink the lemonade and then, when we felt a bit of stiffness starting, we could just swallow a tiny little bit of carrot and we'd be all right again? That way, we could make the carrots last for a really long time, couldn't we?"

Everybody stared at Measle, their faces blank. Measle began to wish he hadn't opened his mouth.

Then Frank smiled. "Wow," he said. "You may be small but you certainly are bright. We could last a long time with that idea."

"Yes, very well done, Measle," said Lady Grant, in her grand voice. "Such a pity that carrots are so revolting, but I suppose we'll have to make the best of it. Perhaps we might wash them first, though?"

"And we don't need to drink lemonade," said Measle. "Basil put in one of those water towers, to fill the boilers of the steam engines. We could drink from that, couldn't we?"

"We certainly could," said Kip. "How come you're so clever?"

Everybody gazed admiringly at Measle and Measle felt his face going red again. He wasn't used to being thought clever. Basil always made a point of telling him how stupid he was and, until now, Measle had believed him. It *had* been pretty stupid to think he could get away with playing with the train set—and yet, here were all these good people telling him that he was clever. The fact was (although Measle didn't know it) Measle *was* pretty clever, with a quick brain and a head crammed with ideas all bursting to come out. There was one thought already bothering him, and he decided to set it free.

"I'm sorry," he said, "but there's something I don't understand. Frank told me not to eat the doughnut crumbs or drink the lemonade. Surely you all told each other the same thing, didn't you? I mean, while you could still talk?"

"We did," said Frank.

"Then why did you all do it anyway?"

"Starvation," said Frank. "It does funny things to you. You get so hungry, you don't care anymore."

Prudence said, "I'm told it happens to people when their ship sinks and they're left in a lifeboat with no water. They know that drinking seawater will kill them, but most of them eventually do it anyway. Same story here."

Everybody nodded gloomily. Then Kip looked up at

the distant rafters. "It's time we got under cover," he said. "It's almost dark."

They all stared fearfully up at the rafters. Prudence said, "Oh my. I'd forgotten. It didn't bother us when we were plastic, but now—"

"Now we're in danger again," said Kip, gathering up his tool bag. "We'd better get out of here."

"But where?" said Prudence.

For some reason, they all looked at Measle, as if they were expecting him to come up with the answer. Since Measle didn't yet know what it was that they were frightened of—and he didn't know the best place to hide—he shrugged his shoulders and looked at the ground, hoping that somebody else would answer.

"Somewhere strong," said Lady Grant decisively. "Somewhere well built. I think I know just the place." She pointed across the town, toward the square. "I used to hide in the town hall—well, it was the only building in this revolting place that even *faintly* resembled my own house, you see. Anyway, I know the structure is quite sound. It's got a good roof and the walls are solid. I don't think it can get at us in there."

"What's 'it'?" asked Measle nervously.

Kitty Webb began to cry softly. Tinker, who had been sitting quietly next to Prudence, got up and trotted over to the girl. He peered into her face and then swiped his tongue over her cheeks, and Kitty found herself smiling through her tears. Tinker (who thought human tears were just another tasty treat) tried another lick. *Nice and salty, these bits of water,* he thought. *Keep 'em coming, little girl!* But Prudence clucked her tongue and pushed Tinker away gently. She put her arm around Kitty and said, "It didn't get you before, because you were very good at hiding. We all were. And we're going to go on being good at hiding, aren't we? I think Lady Grant's suggestion is an excellent one. I hid there myself quite often and it never got to me, did it?"

Measle wondered why nobody had answered his question. He decided to ask again later. In the meantime, he followed the rest of the group as they walked quickly through the darkening streets. Soon they reached the square. As they passed the statue, he turned to Prudence Peyser.

"Do you know what that bit means?" he asked, pointing to the second row of words that were carved into the stone base.

"I do indeed," said Prudence. "The great Roman leader Julius Caesar said it when he conquered Gaul. '*Veni, vidi, vici.*' It's Latin. It means, 'I came, I saw, I conquered.'"

"Oh," said Measle.

"A very vain Wrathmonk is our Mr. Tramplebone," said Prudence. "Imagine—comparing himself to Julius Caesar!"

Measle felt a small tug on his hand. He looked down. Kitty was pulling at his arm.

"Come on," she said. "Everybody's waiting."

Measle looked toward the town hall. The others were already on the steps that led to the massive double front doors, and Measle saw Kip and Frank waving urgently in his direction. He turned to Prudence and said, "We ought to go."

Prudence looked up at the gathering shadows and then back to Measle and Kitty. "Yes, yes. Quickly now. There's not a moment to lose."

She grabbed Measle's free hand, and the three of them trotted across the sandpaper grass, up the steps of the town hall and through the dark opening of the great doors.

5

THE THING

The town hall had something in common with the long, low railroad shed near the coal heap. Of course, it was much bigger and from the outside it appeared to have three stories. But inside, it was the same as the shed—completely empty, just a large, square space with a high ceiling and a bare, new-looking plywood floor.

The group picked a corner to settle down in. William sat on his suitcase. Frank put his electrician's toolbox by the wall. Kip stood watching them, his heavy carpenter's bag dangling from one massive hand and his chain saw and the red fuel can from the other.

"It strikes me that we're quite a useful little crowd," he said. "Here we've got a professional electrician, another fellow with a lot of great books. . . . I'm a carpenter and a pretty good one. . . . We've got a lady who knows about Wrathmonks—"

"Just a bit," said Prudence, modestly.

"Well, more than the rest of us," said Kip. "Plus— and it's a *big* plus—we've got somebody with a cool head and a quick brain—"

"You're too kind," murmured Lady Grant.

Kip laughed. "No disrespect, Lady Grant, but I was talking about young Measle here."

"Oh," said Lady Grant. "Well, of course he's very clever. And sweet. And brave. And very dirty, and with a haircut that defies description—but nevertheless, we all owe him a vote of thanks."

Measle felt his face going red again. It seemed to be doing that a lot lately.

Kip said, "We certainly do, Lady Grant. Thank you for reminding us of it. And last but not least, we have a young lady who—if the uniform she's wearing doesn't lie—knows a lot about a whole bunch of things."

So far, Measle thought, little Kitty Webb only seemed to know how to cry. She also seemed to know how to stick herself very close to him—she was there now, right by his side. Measle realized that she hadn't left it since the moment they had revived her.

Kip said, "Yes. A pretty useful bunch. Maybe we could pool our talents. Do something about getting out of here."

Lady Grant sighed. "It's a nice thought," she said. "But let's face facts. We're half an inch tall, we're stuck on a tabletop with no way of getting down from it, at the complete mercy of that terrible, *revolting* thing in the rafters—"

Measle couldn't contain himself any longer.

"What *is* the thing in the rafters?" he said, so loudly that Lady Grant stopped talking immediately. She, along with all the others, looked at Measle for a moment, as if wondering whether to tell him.

Frank said, "We don't like to talk about it, Measle, but I guess you'd better know. You're going to find out sooner or later anyway." He stared at Measle, his face serious. "The thing in the rafters is a bat."

A *bat*? Measle frowned, puzzled. Bats weren't scary at all—at least, not to Measle. They were just cute little furry things that flew about, eating insects and hanging upside down when they were asleep, looking like Basil's umbrella.

Frank saw Measle's frown. "Yes, I know. What's so scary about a bat? Nothing—unless you're half an inch tall. Then they're very scary indeed."

"Horrid, revolting things," said Lady Grant. "No matter what size you are."

"And this one is not a normal bat," said Prudence. "It's certainly not like any bat I've ever seen."

"Nothing like it mentioned in my encyclopedia," said William.

"This one has legs," said Kip. "With talons on the end of them. Like an eagle's. No bat I ever saw had talons."

"Ordinary bats snatch their prey with their mouths," said William. "This one grabs its prey with its great, curved claws and then carries it away. Up into the rafters. A very nasty piece of work, I don't mind telling you. Dear, oh dear, yes. Even worse than my boss."

Kitty began to cry again. She did it very quietly, burying her face in Measle's sleeve. "It comes out at night," she whispered, her voice muffled, so that only Measle heard her. "It comes out at night and eats us."

"It didn't eat *you*," said Measle, hoping that Kitty would stop crying. She was making his shirtsleeve damp.

"It ate lots of the others," said Kitty.

Measle looked at the group of people. They all had very serious faces and some of them were staring at the floor.

Measle said, "There were *others?*"

"About twenty," said Frank. "All sorts of people, from all walks of life. They were the unlucky ones. They got caught by the thing when they were still human, before the plastic took them over."

"You see, once you're plastic, the thing doesn't bother with you," said Kip. "It can't eat plastic."

"Meantime—while you're still human—you hide," said William.

Measle thought about this for a moment. Then he said, "But you were all *outside* when Frank and I found you. So was Frank, when I found *him*. You weren't under cover—so how come the bat didn't get you when you were still human?"

Lady Grant said, "We *were* under cover. All of us,

most of the time. Especially at night, of course. Particularly as we felt ourselves getting stiffer and stiffer. But once we were unable to move at all, that revolting Tramplebone dragged us out of our hiding places with a gigantic pair of tweezers. He very nearly ruined this suit of mine. It's a Chanel, you know— handmade and quite expensive. One simply cannot pull it around the way he did and then expect it to look nice. Anyway, once he'd got us out, he simply placed us wherever he felt like."

"Look," said Frank, quietly. He was pointing toward the window. It was dark outside.

"That thing will be coming out soon," said William. He'd made a kind of chair from his encyclopedias, using two small piles of the books to fashion a pair of armrests for himself, and he was sitting in the contraption, looking comfortable. Measle noticed that the location William had chosen for himself was as far from the windows of the town hall as possible.

"I think I want to see it," said Measle. "I want to see the bat."

"Okay," said Frank. "You'll be safe if you squat down by the window."

"Aren't you going to watch for it, too?" said Measle, hoping for some companionship.

"I've seen it," said Frank. "Too many times. We all have, Measle."

Measle went to one of the tall windows and sat down, his nose just reaching the windowsill. He peered out at the gloom. He could still see the statue in the town square, and the trees that surrounded it, but the houses on the other side of the square were lost in the gathering darkness.

For the first time in a very long while, Measle felt despair creeping over him. His life up until this moment had been pretty miserable, but Measle was not the sort of person to feel sorry for himself. But now, the future seemed very bleak. He wondered how long they could all survive like this. Not long, surely? A few weeks at most, before the sparse number of carrots he had left in the paper bag ran out. And then what? Starvation, followed by a few desperate meals of doughnuts and pink lemonade—and then the creeping paralysis, with them all ending up like the big carpenter, Kip Lovell. Eventually, Measle reasoned, the plastic would take over completely and there would be no more breathing—which meant, he supposed, death. If you couldn't breathe, you died. It was unthinkable. There had to be a way out of this terrible situation.

Then, he heard it. A distant flapping . . . not of wings, which make a soft, feathery sound—no, this was different. There was something hard about this sound, as though the wings of this flying creature were made not of soft feathers but of some kind of stiff leather. There was a distinct *crack, crack, crack* as it came nearer, and Measle thought he could hear a *whoosh*ing sound as the wings beat through the air.

Then there was a shape, high above the town. Even at this distance, Measle could see it was big. He could just make out the wings of the creature, batting back and forth as it circled above the buildings. They were wide and black and menacing—*crack, crack, crack*—and Measle saw that, as the thing flew in wide circles, it was steadily descending toward the square.

"It's coming," he said.

There was no reply from the other side of the room. Measle turned his head and saw that everybody was pressed against the far wall, their eyes wide with fear.

"It can't get in here, can it?" he asked.

"I don't think so," said Lady Grant. Measle could hear the terror in her voice. "I've hidden here lots of times and I'm sure it knew I was here."

Measle turned back to the window, lowering his head so that only his eyes showed over the sill. The bat was making one last, low-level circle above them. It was huge. Now Measle could see the black fur on its underside. He caught a glimpse of the enormous ears, tilted forward and moving from left to right as the creature strained to listen for its prey. Then, with a sudden flurry of wing beats, it landed in the square. For a moment it was still. And then it began to move across the square, toward the town hall.

The way it moved was so alien that Measle closed his eyes for a second, hoping he hadn't seen what he'd seen. Normal bats, he knew, have difficulty moving on land. They have to lie flat and pull themselves along with the little claws on their wings. Not this bat—if it *was* a bat. This creature stood on a pair of scaly legs and walked on them, like a huge bird. There was a scraping sound as its massive talons dragged across the sandpaper grass, then a sudden clatter as a great claw knocked the Bengal tiger to one side. The tiger rolled over several times and then crashed into the base of the statue. The bat took no notice. It came on, its head jerking back and forth, like a walking pigeon.

It was getting close to Measle's window. He lowered his head even farther, until only one eye was still peeking over the edge. There was a strong smell now, too—like the smell of a mouse cage that hasn't been cleaned in a long time.

The bat loomed huge against the window. Its head was taller than the roof of the town hall and it had to bend its body low to put its face to the glass. The enormous head filled the whole space and the eyes—bloodred and slanting upward at the corners—were the size of dinner plates. Its nose looked like a pig's snout, except it was triangular. The tip of the nose wriggled like a pig's, and below the nose, there was a wide, lipless mouth—slightly open, so that Measle could see two rows of needle-sharp yellow teeth. Its breath steamed up the glass on the outside, but through the fog on the window Measle could see that its eyes—just a couple of inches away from where he crouched—were not looking at him. They seemed to be peering into the room, darting this way and that, never focusing on anything in particular.

Tinker barked. Somebody screamed. At first, Measle thought it was Kitty. He turned quickly and saw that the sharp sound of fear had come from Lady Grant. Her hand was over her mouth, and her eyes were wide and staring with terror.

"Sh!" whispered Measle fiercely. "It'll hear us!"

"It's heard us already," hissed Kip. "Its ears are amazing. It can hear our hearts beating."

"Don't let it get me," muttered Lady Grant, through her fingers.

There was a noise behind Measle, and he turned back to the window. *Scritch, scritch, scritch.* One of the bat's long claws was scraping down the glass of the window.

"It's getting in!" yelled William, jerking his arms so violently that the two armrests of his book chair spilled to the floor with a thud.

Lady Grant screamed again.

Scritch, scritch, scritch—

Measle saw, to his horror, that the glass was bending under the pressure from the great claw. He scrambled backward on all fours, until he reached the group that was huddled against the far wall.

"It can smell us, too," whispered Frank. "So many of us, all in one place. And no longer made of plastic. It can't believe its luck."

They waited, holding their breath—

The bending pane of glass cracked with the sound of a pistol shot.

And then light suddenly flooded the darkness. It wasn't sunlight, which has a hard, bright white quality to it; this light was a yellowish color and was far less penetrating, but it was enough for the bat to turn its hideous face away from the window. A moment later, they saw it back away from the building in a hurried, scrambling sort of way. It seemed to crouch for a second. Then, it sprang into the air. They could hear the *crack, crack, crack* of its leathery wings receding into the distance.

Everybody breathed a sigh of relief, and Kitty, who had crawled as close to Measle as she could, said in a small voice, "Has it gone?"

"Looks like it," said Measle. "But where's that light coming from?"

"It's the overhead bulb," said Frank. "The one that hangs down from the ceiling over the train set."

"More trouble," said Kip in a low voice.

"Out of the frying pan, into the fire," said William.

"It's Basil," said Prudence, nervously pushing a lock of gray hair off her forehead. "He's here. And he's going to wonder where we all are."

They waited, listening to the long silence. Then came Basil's voice, like a thunderclap, directly overhead.

"WHAT IS THISSS?"

It was so loud that a little dust that had collected on the ceiling of the town hall was shaken free by the vibration and drifted slowly down through the still air.

"WHAT HAS BEEN GOING ON HERE? WHERE ARE MY SSSPECIAL LITTLE VICTIMS?"

There was another pause and then Basil's voice again, quieter this time, a kind of vicious whisper that sounded like wind whistling in a chimney.

"Thisss is your doing, isn't it, Measle? You've found all my ssspecial little plasssticated victims and you've hidden them sssomewhere, haven't you? Now—where could you have hidden them? And why? There's a quessstion for you—why would you do sssuch a thing? I want my little victims back where they belong,

Measle, ssso why don't you come out of your hiding place and tell me where you've put them? I won't hurt you, Measle, not if you're quick. Come along, now—show yoursssself."

"What should I do?" whispered Measle.

"Stay put," muttered Frank. "He doesn't know where you are, and he's not going to tear his beloved train set apart to find you."

"I wonder about sssomething," hissed Basil's voice. "I wonder why—when I came in and ssswitched on the light—why my little furry friend jussst happened to be peering in through the windows of the town hall? Why would Cuddlebug be doing that, do you sssuppose? That'sss his name, you know—Cuddlebug. Sssuch a dear little chap. He and I are the very bessst of friends. He keepsss thisss place ssso clean—not a living thing in sssight! Could it be that Cuddlebug knows sssomething that I don't? Could it be that there's sssomething *hiding* in the town hall? Sssomething that Cuddlebug would like to eat? Hmmm? Well, I shall have to get my flashlight, won't I? I shall have to shine it into the town hall and sssee what there is to be sssseen."

They heard Basil moving away. Measle knew where

the flashlight was. It hung on a hook, right beside the attic door.

"He's going to be back in a second!" he said urgently. "What are we going to do?"

"He mustn't know we're alive," said Prudence. "There's no telling what he'd do to us."

"Quick, everybody!" said Frank. "Get into the same positions—the ones we were in when we were plastic! It's our only hope! Measle, try and hide behind us! Come on, everybody, huddle close together!"

Within a few seconds, everybody had crowded together and adopted their statue positions. Lady Grant was crouched huddling on the floor, William was posed as if running for his life, Kitty had her arms wrapped tight round an imaginary pine tree—all positioned as Basil had set them. All except Tinker, who, being a dog, couldn't understand what was going on. He whined and pushed his nose against stiff hands, trying to nuzzle everybody back to life.

"Grab him, Measle!" said Frank. "Try to keep him quiet!"

Measle took hold of Tinker's collar and pulled him into the narrow space behind the grouped figures. He crouched down, his back to the wall, pulling Tinker down next to him. He put his hand around Tinker's nose and whispered, "Be quiet now, Tinker. That's a good boy. Not a sound, Tinker."

The little dog seemed to sense the urgency in Measle's voice and lay quietly by his side, his head on his paws. He quite liked the smelly kid's hand on his nose. The smelly kid's hand was nice and grubby and smelled very interesting. *A bit too much scent of that nasty orange rooty thing that they shoved down my throat earlier,* he thought. *But the rest is very appealing. Mixture of soot and sweat and friendly boy—and a trace of donut in there, too—yup, very pleasant indeedydoody. . . .*

They all heard Basil's footsteps, coming closer. They all saw the beam of bright light flashing across the tall windows of the town hall. They all heard his voice. "Now then. Let usss sssee what ssso interesssted my little furry friend."

A blinding light flooded over them and Frank whispered, through clenched teeth, "Everybody be still! Not a twitch from anybody!"

There was a gap of about a quarter of an inch between Lady Grant and William, and Measle could see the window through it. He was in deep shadow and felt sure that Basil wouldn't be able to catch sight of him, so he felt safe in peering through the narrow gap. He kept a firm hand on Tinker's nose. He saw the flashlight sweeping across the window, and then he saw Basil's enormous eye next to it.

"Well, well, well," said Basil. "There they are. One, two, three, four, five, sssix. All present and correct. No—I'm missstaken. Where is the little dog? And where is young Measle? What a puzzle it is, to be sssure. All my tiny victims—but no dog and no Measle. Perhapsss you've been eaten, Measle? Is that it? Did my furry friend get you? Did Cuddlebug carry you off to his lair in the rafters? Hmmm—on sssecond thought, I think not. Not you, Measle. No, you're far too crafty for that, aren't you? Ssso, where are you? And where's the dog? Are you together, perhapsss? Are you hiding sssomeplace elssse, with a plassstic dog for a companion? How sssad, Measle. You and a little plassstic dog."

Basil's enormous eye withdrew and, a moment later, the bright beam of the flashlight disappeared, plunging them back into semidarkness. Now there was only the sickly light from the bare overhead bulb.

Basil's voice, high above them now, boomed, "Well, we shall look for you tomorrow, Measle. Tomorrow, in daytime, when the light is better. And we shall get our long tweezers and we shall take all my little victims out of the town hall and put them back where they belong. And we shall find you, Measle. We shall find you and your plassstic dog and we shall punish you for re-arranging my train ssset—because nobody but me is allowed to play with my train ssset, Measle. Nobody but me. *In* it, yesss. *With* it, no. Good night—and sssleep tight."

Basil sniggered. Then there was the *thud, thud, thud* of Basil's heavy footsteps moving toward the door. A *click* of a switch and the yellow light disappeared, fol-lowed by the distinct thump as the attic door was closed. Everybody was still. Only when they heard the distant sound of Basil moving down the attic staircase did they drop their posed positions and relax.

"We've got a problem," said Frank. "A worse prob-lem than we had before. We've got to hide young Measle, so that Basil can't find him. In fact, we've *all* got to hide—we can't keep up the statue act, not in broad daylight—but Measle has to hide most of all. We need him and there's no telling what that Wrathmonk would do to him."

Lady Grant sniffed. "But there's nowhere to hide. You know that. I mean, it's a big table, certainly—but that revolting Tramplebone could examine every inch of it in a few minutes."

"Besides," said William, "we can't leave this place. Not at night. Not with that thing on the hunt for us. And my books can't help with a thing like that."

"There's nowhere for us to go," whimpered Lady Grant.

There was a long, gloomy silence. Then Kitty whispered in Measle's ear, "We could be like termites."

"What?" said Measle.

"Termites. You hardly ever see termites."

"What was that, dear?" said Prudence.

Kitty looked at Measle, as though she was asking him to explain to the rest of them.

"She said something about termites," Measle muttered.

"Termites?" said Lady Grant, sounding irritable. "What is the dear girl talking about? What are termites?"

"Ah well, now—according to the encyclopedia, they're a kind of ant," said William, in the sort of voice people use when they've learned something by heart. "Their main diet is wood. In the process of eating it, they can produce extensive burrows. They live in large colonies. There is a queen, who lays eggs—"

"Oh," said Kip, slowly. "Now there's an idea."

"*What* idea?" said Lady Grant. "What are we talking about *ants* for?"

Kip smiled. "Not ants. *Termites*. Termites burrow. They make tunnels in wood—long, twisting tunnels, which keep them safe, out of sight. Out of harm's way. I should know—I've seen enough evidence of them in my line of work."

"How horrid for you," said Lady Grant crossly. "But what have they got to do with us?"

"Everything," said Kip. He turned to Kitty. "You're a very clever girl."

6

THE
TUNNEL

They dug all night.

Kip started the process by cutting, with his thinnest saw, through the top layer of a square piece of plywood. He chose a section of flooring in the farthest corner from the door and windows, and his saw cut was so fine that, when the piece was replaced, it was hard to see where the cut was. Then he used an iron crowbar to lever the thin sliver of wood off the floor. This was to be their trapdoor. Once that was done, all three men began to saw and drill and chisel their way downward, using the tools that Kip and Frank had in their kits.

The idea was to burrow down into the plywood, cutting first a pit big enough so that even the largest among them could fit into it. Then they would begin to dig sideways, carving out a horizontal tunnel. At first there was nothing for Measle, Kitty, Lady Grant and Prudence to do. But soon a pile of wood chips had grown by the side of the excavation and the question arose: Where to put the debris?

"Basil's sure to see that," said Kip. Sweat was running down his face.

"We shall have to hide it somewhere," said Prudence. "But where?"

They looked around the big room. There was no place that wasn't visible through the tall windows—except, perhaps, for a narrow section immediately beneath the windowsills.

"If we spread the stuff along the wall here," said Kip, "there's a chance that he won't be able to see it without removing the whole building—and I don't think he'll do that."

Now Measle, Kitty, Prudence and Lady Grant had a job to do. They collected armfuls of the debris and spread it along the wall beneath the windows of the room. At first Lady Grant carefully brushed the sawdust off her Chanel suit after every trip, but she soon gave that up and hardly complained at all.

It took most of the night before the pit was dug deep enough to allow them to start the horizontal tunnel, and the pile of debris that Measle and his helpers had cleared away was almost up to the bottoms of the windowsills.

Frank was standing in the pit. His head just reached level with the top. He stopped drilling for a moment and said, "How thick is this plywood, Kip?"

"Three quarters of an inch. Why?"

"Well, if we're half an inch tall—most of us, anyway—that means there's only a quarter of an inch left under our feet. It seems to me that it might be an idea to keep going until we break through."

"Break through?" said William dubiously. "We could all fall to nasty, sticky deaths."

Frank shook his head. "Not if we're careful, William. My idea is this: if we could cut a small hole down at the bottom of this pit—and make sure it wasn't so big that somebody could fall through—then we'd have a way of disposing of the rest of the debris."

"I think you've got something there," said Kip. "We're so far from the ground that the stuff is sure to disperse on the way down. I don't think it would form much of a heap, so Basil may not notice anything."

They attacked the wood and, twenty minutes later, Kip said, "Hold it. We're there."

He sent the other two men out of the pit and then, carefully, he chiseled out a small hole. He gathered some wood chips and dropped them through the small opening, watching them drift down through the still air and noticing, with satisfaction, that they scattered over the distant floor below, so as to be almost unnoticeable.

"Well, it works," he called, and everybody clustered around the top of the tunnel. Looking down made Measle dizzy. The floor of the attic seemed hundreds, even thousands, of feet beneath him.

"Now we can start work on the tunnel," said Kip. "We'll make regular holes in the bottom, just like this one. That way, we can get rid of the chips and get breathing air at the same time. Come on, everybody—back to work."

Measle, Lady Grant, Prudence and Kitty went back

to the surface while the three men set to work. They talked a little until one by one they fell asleep. Only Measle stayed awake. Sometime during the early hours of the morning, Measle heard the *crack, crack, crack* of the huge bat's wings as it flew overhead. The others started awake at the sound.

"It's come back from hunting," said Prudence.

"Back from where?"

"From outside. It checks out the attic first and eats anything that moves. That's why there aren't any insects up here. Then it flies out through the broken window and comes back shortly before dawn." Prudence looked at her watch. "There you are—it's five o'clock in the morning. It'll be light soon."

"Where is the creature now?" asked Measle nervously.

"Back in its roost up in the rafters. It'll sleep now until night comes again."

Prudence went to the pit and called down, "It's almost dawn, boys. How are you doing?"

William popped his head out of the tunnel. He was covered in sawdust and wood chips, and he looked very tired. "Not bad for a slightly overweight encyclopedia salesman," he said. "Come and have a look."

112

Measle went first, dropping down into the pit. William moved to one side, and Measle peered into the tunnel. He could see Kip and Frank at the far end, still chipping and drilling and sawing at the wooden surface. The tunnel was about two and a half inches long.

"That's brilliant," said Measle, meaning it.

Prudence climbed down, with the help of William. "How long before Basil comes back?" she asked.

"He always sleeps pretty late," said Measle. "I reckon we're safe until nine o'clock."

William looked at his watch. "Another four hours. We can dig a lot farther in four hours."

The three men kept going. As soon as it was light, Measle, Lady Grant, Prudence and Kitty went out in search of food and drink. Measle led them to the spot near the rail yards where he'd found Frank, and they stuffed Lady Grant's handbag with doughnut crumbs. Lady Grant started to tell them that her handbag was extremely expensive, having been made for her by an exclusive firm in Rome, Italy, and that perhaps doughnut crumbs were not the most appropriate objects to put into such a costly creation, but Prudence cut her short by saying, "Now come along, dear—there isn't time for all that." Lady Grant went a little pink and closed her mouth and said nothing more. She followed meekly as they walked quickly along the railway tracks to the water tower.

Frank had given Measle a plastic bucket and Measle climbed up the ladder on the side of the tower and dipped the bucket into the water. He passed it down to Prudence, and then climbed back down himself.

"This should last us awhile," said Prudence.

They hurried back to the town hall. Inside, the men were taking a break. All three were hot and dusty and very thirsty, and they drank the water and ate the doughnut crumbs with gratitude. When they had finished, Measle took the smallest piece of carrot from the paper bag and cut four little chips from it and gave one to each man.

"I hope this works," said William, swallowing his carrot chip in one gulp.

Frank said, "It's eight thirty. We ought to hide now, just to be on the safe side."

One by one, they dropped down into the pit. Kip went last, bringing a protesting Tinker with him. He pulled the square sheet of plywood over his head, fitting it exactly over the hole. "Let's hope Basil doesn't notice the cut," he said.

Frank said, "That's as fine a cut as I've ever seen. And remember, it's pretty dark inside the town hall, even with Basil's flashlight. I don't think he'll see a thing."

Measle had expected complete darkness once the cover had been put in place, but the little hole at the bottom of the pit let in a small amount of light, so they were able to see the tunnel entrance. They all crawled into the rough burrow. It was now three inches long— more than enough room for all of them. There was another small hole drilled into the floor of the tunnel, near the spot where it ended, and the light from this allowed them to see one another clearly.

"What now?" said Lady Grant.

"Now we wait," said Frank.

They didn't have to wait long. Soon they heard Basil's heavy tread coming up the attic stairs—then the creak of the attic door—then Basil's booming voice, muffled now by the quarter inch of plywood over their heads.

"Good morning, Measle. I trussst you ssslept well? I

have my tweezers, dear boy. Once I've replaced my ssspecial little victims, I shall come looking for you. And when I find you, I think I shall turn you into sssomething even more unpleasant than what you are now—a dirty, disssobedient little creature. An insssect, perhapsss? Yesss—a nasssty, dirty insssect."

Measle shivered and Prudence put her arm around his shoulders. "Don't listen to him," she whispered. "He won't do anything to you. We shan't let him."

Measle didn't see how they could stop Basil doing whatever he wanted, but it was kind of Prudence to pretend that they could. He remembered something that she'd said the day before, and a tiny seed of an idea began to germinate in his brain. He kept quiet, because the idea wasn't yet fully formed in his mind—

The roar shook their tunnel.

"WHAT IS THISSS? WHAT IS GOING ON? WHERE ARE THEY ALL?"

The roar became a low rumble of rage—but through the anger in Basil's voice, Measle thought he detected a slight tone of uneasiness, as though Basil, for the first time in his mad and evil life, had met with something he couldn't understand.

"Oh, Measle—you wicked, wicked boy. What have you done with my little plassstic victims? Where have you put them, eh? And why? Well, we shall find them, make no missstake about that. They can't have gone far, can they? Not with legs as ssstiff as theirs. And neither can you. And when I find you, yesss—definitely an insssect. A cockroach, perhapsss."

They heard Basil moving slowly around the great table. Sometimes the wood that surrounded them creaked when Basil leaned his great weight on it, and once their tunnel shook, as though in an earthquake, when Basil bumped the edge of the table with his hip. Then they heard the thump of his footsteps returning.

"Very clever, Measle. Mossst ingeniousss. I confess—I've looked everywhere and my victims are nowhere to be ssseen. Not on the table, not on the floor. Ssso—what have you done with them? And all by yourssself, too. Mossst impresssive, Measle. And now I am very angry. Very angry indeed. And do you know what I do when I am very angry indeed? I don't get hot, like sssome angry people do. No—I get very cold. As cold as ice. Like thisss."

Measle shivered again—but this time, not from fear.

There was an icy chill coming up through the hole in the tunnel floor. He looked at the others, huddled in the dim light, and he saw that their breath was coming out of their mouths in clouds of steam.

"What's happening?" whispered Lady Grant.

"It's Basil," said Prudence, her teeth beginning to chatter. "He's making it cold."

"We can't survive this for long," said Frank, bundling his blue coat around him. "We'll freeze to death."

Kip said, "If it's this cold in here, it's a lot colder out there. Wood is a great insulator."

"I don't feel very insulated," said William. "My bones are beginning to ache."

Tinker whined softly. He could feel a film of ice forming on his wet nose. *This is no good, no good at all. How am I expected to smell anything with a rotten great iceberg on my snout?* He shuffled around and pushed his nose against Measle's jacket. *Ah—much better—but now my toes are beginning to freeze!* He tucked his stumpy legs under his body and huddled closer to the smelly kid.

Measle could feel little Kitty shivering next to him and he wondered if her tears would turn to ice. Then, a moment later, the cold began to decrease. The icy wind whistling up through the hole began to slacken off, and soon the temperature was back to normal. Then Basil's voice boomed out again.

"Cold enough for you, was it, Measle? Well, tomorrow it will be much colder. That was jussst a tassste of what'sss to come, Measle. Tomorrow it will be ten times colder—and for much, much longer. At the end, you'll be frozen sssolid, like an ice cube. And that means you'll be dead, Measle. Unless, of courssse, I find all my little victims back where they belong. Then I won't freeze you sssolid, Measle. No, I shall jussst turn you into a nasssty little cockroach, and you can ssscuttle about the tabletop for as long as you like. Or, at leassst, for as long as Cuddlebug will let you. Which will it be, Measle? Death by freezing—or life as a cockroach? I know which one I would choose. There's a sssaying, Measle: 'Where there's life, there's hope.' Choose wisely. Ssso—until tomorrow, Measle."

There was the familiar *thump, thump, thump* as Basil moved away to the attic door. A creak—and then the sound of the door closing, followed by the *thump, thump, thump* as Basil descended the stairs.

For a long time, everybody sat in silence. Then

Measle said, "I'm sorry."

"What for?" said Prudence.

"For all this. Putting you all in danger."

"Measle," said Frank, putting both his hands on Measle's shoulders, "there's nothing to be sorry about. Basil's right about one thing. Where there's life, there's hope. You brought us back to life, and that means you gave us hope."

"And we've got twenty-four hours to think of something," said Kip.

"What if we plug up the holes?" asked William. "You said wood is a good insulator."

Kip shook his head. "It's good, but not that good. Not against that kind of cold."

"And if we plug up the holes, we'll run out of air pretty fast," said Frank.

"What I don't understand," said Lady Grant, "is why that revolting creature didn't freeze us all solid there and then. Why wait until tomorrow?"

"I'm fairly sure," said Prudence, slowly, "that Basil can only do one major spell every twenty-four hours. It takes a lot of energy to do a major spell like that freezing one."

"You know about the spells?" asked Frank. "Do you know how he does them?"

"Heavens, no," said Prudence. "And it's all theory, really. But from my observations of Wizards and Warlocks and Wrathmonks, it does seem that there's a limit to their abilities. Big spells, like chilling a whole room down to subzero temperatures—well, they take some doing. Besides, Basil wants us all back where he put us and he wants Measle to do it—and Measle can't do it if he's frozen, can he?"

Measle was thinking hard. The idea he'd had a few minutes before was growing fast. Prudence had said that a Wrathmonk's spell was stronger than the Wrathmonk. Then, perhaps—what if the direction of a spell could somehow be changed—

Measle took a deep breath. Then he said, "I think we should let Basil turn me into a cockroach."

"What?" said Lady Grant, her mouth dropping open in astonishment. "Why on earth would we want to let him do that?"

"No, Measle," said Frank. "No—we can't let that happen to you."

"Besides," said Lady Grant, with a shudder, "I hate

cockroaches. Ugly, revolting things."

Measle shook his head. He turned to Prudence and said, "Look, if you're right, there's a good chance he won't succeed. It's risky, but it might just work—and anyway, there's nothing else we can do."

Then he told them his idea.

7

THE
REBELLION

It wasn't a long walk to the little house by the lake. It took them ten minutes to reach it.

The house—it was more of a cabin, really—stood deep in the shadow of the trees that surrounded it. It was made of logs and was small; once they were inside, there was little room to move around. It had one advantage over the town hall: there was only one tiny window, far too small for the bat to get through. The cabin also appeared to be well built, and they felt pretty sure that it could withstand any number of attacks from the monster—if it ever discovered they were inside.

Once they had made camp in the cabin, Measle led the way to the lake. It was nothing more than a mirror, cleverly cut in a random shape so as to resemble a small body of water set deep in the forest. It was fixed into the plywood surface of the table and surrounded by low banks of green-painted sandpaper, which looked remarkably like grass.

Kip, Frank and William set to work. Using crowbars from the tool kits, they began to loosen the mirror from its setting, being careful not to crack the thin glass. It took a long time, pushing the bladed ends of the crowbars under the lip of the glass, bit by bit, and gently easing it out of its setting. Shortly before it got dark, Kip and Frank gave one last heave, and with a crackling sound, they lifted one edge of the mirror, tilting the whole thing up at a narrow angle. Then the rest of them, except for Measle, ran forward and took hold of a section of the mirror.

"All right," shouted Kip. "All together now! Lift!"

Everybody strained their muscles and one side of the mirror lifted clear from its setting—a whole quarter of an inch.

It was enough. Measle quickly crawled forward and fit his thin body in the narrow gap between the underside of the mirror and the plywood tabletop. Tinker thought this was some new kind of game and crawled in beside him. Measle gently pushed him away. "No, Tinker," he said. "Go away, there's a good dog." Then he crawled backward onto the sandpaper bank and, with a collective sigh of relief, the others lowered the mirror back into place.

"Well, it ought to work," said Frank.

"But it's a terrible risk, Measle dear," said Prudence. "Remember, it's only a theory. It could all go badly wrong."

Measle grinned at her, pretending to be brave. He was, in fact, very frightened by his idea—but it seemed that there was nothing else they could try. He busied himself helping the men to cut some short lengths of wood. Kip cut down a small tree with his chain saw, and they chopped the trunk into half-inch pieces. Then they took the sections of timber to the lakeside. Once again, the men levered the mirror up. Lady Grant and Prudence joined in, to hold the side of the mirror clear, while Measle and Kitty propped the lengths of wood under the glass. Once they'd set the first three in place, Kip said, "Okay—lower away."

Slowly, gently, they lowered the mirror onto the props. Then they set the remaining sections of timber around the edge of the glass, until Kip was satisfied that the thing was steady and firm.

"Do you think Basil will notice?" asked Prudence.

"He'd have to look pretty closely to see it's not flat," said Kip.

"Let's hope he doesn't look closely," said William.

"Let's hope he'll be looking at me," said Measle.

"Oh dear," said Prudence. "I do worry about this."

They returned to the cabin just as the light from the broken attic window began to fade. They all went inside the cramped area, closed the door and settled down on the floor.

William said, "I've had a tiny thought. To match my tiny brain." He turned to Prudence and Lady Grant. "Do either of you two ladies have any perfume in your handbags?"

Prudence shook her head. "Never use the stuff."

Lady Grant said, "I've got some. Why?"

"I want to try something," said William. "I want to mask our smells with something else. I read in my books that if you make yourself smell of something else, animals that rely on their sense of smell sometimes get confused. It seems to me that if we spray ourselves—and this room—with some good, strong perfume, perhaps the bat might leave us alone."

"It's worth a try," said Frank.

Lady Grant rummaged in her handbag and pulled out a small square bottle, with a spray cap. She dusted some doughnut crumbs off it and said, "This is very expensive. It's called Jolie Femme. I do hope you're not going to use all of it?"

William smiled. "Lady Grant," he said, "if we ever get out of this mess, I'll buy you a case of the stuff."

Lady Grant smiled faintly. "That is terribly sweet of you," she murmured. "But I'm afraid you wouldn't be able to afford a whole case. I don't know *anybody*— except me, of course—who could afford a whole case."

William grinned and took the bottle and began spraying everything in the room—the walls, the little window, the door and Tinker, who sneezed and wiped his eyes with his paws. *That's the kind of stink,* he thought, *that a self-respecting dog can do without, thank you very much!* Then William used what was left in the bottle to spray everybody's clothes—Measle most of all, because Measle had the strongest smell.

"You ever hear of a bathtub, kiddo?" he said, grinning, as he squirted Measle's dirty old shirt.

"Have you ever seen my bathwater?" said Measle, wrinkling his nose against the strong scent. "If you had, you wouldn't take a bath either."

Soon the darkness came and with it the *crack, crack, crack* of the great bat wings. They heard it flying over the cabin, the sound getting closer and closer. Then there was a thump as the bat landed—and a rustling noise as it pushed its way through the trees.

"It's coming," whispered Kitty.

They all huddled together, holding their breath.

They could hear a snuffling right outside the door—then, in quick succession, three short, sharp sneezes. A moment later, they heard a sudden *whoosh* of wind and then—*crack, crack, crack* as the bat took off.

"It didn't like that," said Frank. "Good idea, William."

"Yes, a *very* good idea, Mr. Durham," said Lady Grant. "A rather *expensive* idea—but a very good one all the same."

"With any luck, it won't be back tonight," said Frank.

They slept that night, some more soundly than others. Measle lay awake for a long time. It wasn't very comforting thinking about the three possible fates that lay ahead. Death by freezing. A short life as a cockroach. Or, with a great deal of luck, the one remaining possibility . . .

Measle fell asleep at last, an hour before dawn. A moment later (or so it seemed) Frank shook him awake.

"It's time, Measle. Are you sure you want to go through with this?"

Measle nodded. He wasn't sure at all, but he knew he had no choice. Prudence hugged him, Lady Grant kissed the air somewhere near his cheek and Kitty began to cry. The three men solemnly shook his hand.

"However this comes out, Measle," said Frank, "we want you to know that we think a lot of you."

"You're a brave kid," said Kip.

"Knock 'em dead," said William.

Measle gulped. Suddenly, it seemed like a terrible idea. He looked around at all the worried faces. They were relying on him. This was no time to back down.

"Okay," he said, his voice strong. "Here I go."

He walked out of the cabin and heard the door close behind him. He made his way through the trees to the edge of the mirror lake. It was just as they'd left it the night before—tilted up on one edge, leaving a gap of a quarter of an inch between it and the plywood base. Measle tried to imagine how it would look from above. The angle of the tilt was very small; with luck, Basil wouldn't notice it.

He sat down on the sandpaper bank to wait. He felt very lonely and very nervous—and horribly exposed. A whole mob of butterflies seemed to be having a party in his stomach and his mouth felt as dry as dust.

The seconds ticked by—then the minutes—then a whole hour had come and gone, and still no Basil. Measle began to hope that perhaps he'd never come. Perhaps he'd decided to leave the house forever? Perhaps he'd conveniently died in his sleep? Perhaps he'd—

Thump, thump, thump. Basil was coming up the stairs. Measle stood up, trembling. His knees started to knock together and he suddenly felt weak. He forced his unwilling legs to take him to the edge of the mirror, and he looked toward the distant door, waiting for the terror that was approaching.

The door opened and Basil was there—huge and towering, his white face whiter than usual, his eyes more staring than ever and strands of his lank, greasy black hair hanging over his high white forehead as if, in his hurry to get his revenge, he'd forgotten to use a comb. Measle watched as Basil walked slowly to the edge of the table. He stood quite still, waiting for Basil to see him.

And then Basil did see him. His great round eyes narrowed and he smiled his terrible smile. He moved around the table to the point closest to Measle, and he leaned both his waxy hands on the surface and lowered his massive head.

"Ssso—there you are, Measle. Taking a little ssstroll in the woods, are we? Fresh air and exersssise—ssso good for the lungs, aren't they? Now, let me try to remember—what were we going to do with you? Ah, yesss—we were going to freeze you sssolid, weren't we?"

Measle blinked. What about the other spell—the cockroach threat? He thought as fast as he'd ever thought.

"I don't care if you freeze me solid!" he shouted. "Just don't turn me into a cockroach!"

"*Don't* turn you into a cockroach? What do you mean, 'don't'? We don't sssay 'don't' to Basil, surely?"

"I don't care what you do to me—just, please, *please* don't turn me into a cockroach!"

"There's that 'don't' again, Measle."

"And I mean it!" shouted Measle, at the top of his lungs. "Don't, don't, *don't* turn me into a cockroach!"

"Ah—ssso, that's what we fear the mossst, is it?"

"Yes! I couldn't bear being a cockroach!"

"Very well, dear boy. Then—a cockroach it shall be! Ssstand quite ssstill, Measle."

Even through his fear, Measle couldn't help feeling a small satisfaction at the success of his ruse, and it occurred to him that Basil's madness had a shrinking effect on his intelligence. Basil leaned forward on his hands and lowered his head closer to where Measle was standing. Then he narrowed his round fish eyes. Measle tensed, concentrating on Basil's dark pupils. The moment he saw the glint of green fire in those fishy orbs, he dived, in one smooth movement, under the tilted mirror.

Basil followed the sudden, unexpected movement of the boy and, at the precise moment when the twin beams of green light flashed from his eyes, he found himself looking directly into the reflecting surface of the mirror. The lime-green rays hit the mirror and bounced at the speed of light right back into Basil's eyes. He screamed—whether from pain or fear, Measle didn't know—and there was a sizzling sound, like bacon frying in a hot pan. Measle huddled under the edge of the mirror. Something was happening out there—but what?

The sizzling noise stopped.

Silence—then an odd scrabbling, clicking sort of sound, coming from a long way away. Measle cautiously crawled out from beneath the mirror and looked up. Basil had gone—disappeared. It was as though he'd never been there and all was quiet—apart from the scrabbling, clicking sound in the distance.

There were too many trees between Measle and the noise. There was only one way to find out what was making it: Measle picked a nearby pine tree, with lots of strong branches at regular intervals all the way up the trunk. He began to climb it. It was lucky he'd chosen a tall one; quite near the top, he found himself looking out over the canopy of the forest. He could see all the way to the edge of the table—and what he saw made his blood run cold.

There, far in the distance, clinging to the edge of the table with its two front legs, was a gigantic, jet-black cockroach. It was at least four inches long. Its antennae were waving frantically and it was trying desperately to heave the rest of its body up onto the table. As Measle watched in horror, the creature made one last effort and slowly pulled its huge body over the edge. Once it was safe, on level ground, it paused for a moment, its antennae waving back and forth, as if it was getting its bearings. Then it turned in Measle's direction and began to move slowly across the tabletop toward him.

Measle shimmied down the pine tree as fast as he could. When he reached the bottom, he raced back to the cabin and threw open the door.

"Quick, everybody! We've got to get out of here! It's coming!"

"What's coming?" said Frank. "Did it work?"

Measle gasped, "It worked okay. It worked really well. That's the trouble. Come on! There's no time to lose!"

"Where are we going now?" said Lady Grant, not moving from her corner of the cabin.

"We've got to get back to the tunnel!" shouted Measle. "It's the only safe place now! Come *on*!"

There was such authority in Measle's voice that they all got to their feet without another word. Prudence snatched up Tinker, and together, they crowded out of the cabin, with Measle leading the way.

The giant insect was delayed momentarily by the thick forest between it and the cabin, but it skirted the trees and headed fast after them. Measle and the others raced through the trees, burst out of the wood and made for the outskirts of the town. As the group neared the buildings, they could hear scrabbling noises close behind them. Nobody dared to look back—the sound of the creature was terrifying enough to keep them all running as fast as they could. They tore along the empty streets, with Prudence huffing and puffing in the rear. At one point, she stumbled and almost fell— but Kip put out one big hand and steadied her. Too tired to speak, Prudence nodded her thanks and they ran on, dodging around corners, their breath rasping in their throats. At last they reached the square, with the town hall on the far side. They dodged past a small group of plastic townspeople, then on past the statue, hearing the clicking and scrabbling coming closer and closer. Measle glanced back and saw the cockroach just turning the corner. He saw the creature barge straight through the group of plastic figures, sending them flying right and left. It grabbed one of the figures in its jaws—the figure was of a boy, about Measle's age and size—and, with a crunch, the great jaws slammed together. The cockroach shook the whole front section of its body, like a wet dog emerging from a bath—and the two halves of the plastic boy flew to either side of the monster, the neatly cut sections skittering and sliding across the sandpaper grass.

It seemed to be saying, *That's what I shall do to you when I catch you, Measle!* Measle gulped in horror.

"Come on, Measle!" screamed Frank, and Measle

turned away from the terrible sight and raced for the town hall. At the great open doors, friendly hands grabbed him and pulled him into the safety of the room. Then those same hands heaved the doors shut with a bang.

They'd made it with inches to spare.

"What is that revolting thing?" panted Lady Grant, staring in horror through the tall window at the approaching monster.

"That's Basil," Measle gasped. "And he's really, *really* angry."

"Come on, everybody," said Frank, herding them all toward the pit in the corner of the room. "It's not safe out here. We've got to get into the tunnel."

They hurried down into the pit, just as the giant cockroach reached the front door of the town hall. They crawled into the tunnel and huddled together at the far end.

"What happened back there?" said Frank, when he'd caught his breath.

"Basil was leaning on the table," said Measle. "So he didn't end up on the floor like we'd hoped. When the spell got directed back at him, I think his hands turned into insect claws and he managed to hang on to the edge of the table and then pull himself up." He looked around at the frightened faces. "I'm sorry—I guess we're in even worse trouble now."

"I don't think so," wheezed Prudence. "I'd rather have to deal with an oversized insect than with Basil."

"Me too," said William. "Apart from anything else, there's the size difference. A four-inch cockroach is bad, but a full-sized Basil is worse. As bad as my boss."

"At least we know that your theory was right," Frank said, smiling at Prudence.

Prudence didn't look happy. "I've just remembered something," she said quietly. "You see, there's a second part to that theory."

"A second part?" said Frank.

"Yes. It's generally believed that a spell that's turned back on itself loses a certain amount of power."

"It doesn't seem to have lost anything," said Frank. "Basil tried to turn Measle into a cockroach, and now he's one himself. I think it worked fine. Of course, it's much bigger than we'd hoped—"

"It's not the effectiveness of the spell that's changed," said Prudence, shaking her head. "It's the duration. A

weakened spell has a time limit. Twenty-four hours—
or so it's believed—and then it wears off . . ."

"Well, okay," said Frank, smiling. "That gives us
some time to come up with something—"

Then he stopped smiling because, overhead, there
was the sound of wood splintering, and plaster crum-
bling, and bricks falling.

"What's happening now?" said Lady Grant. There
was a trace of panic in her voice.

"I think it just pushed its way into the town hall,"
said Frank.

"Like a bulldozer," said William. "A battering ram."

"It can't get at us, can it?" said Lady Grant.

"I don't think so," said Kip. "Plywood is strong stuff."

They heard something scraping over the floor above
their heads. A shaft of light appeared at the end of the
tunnel.

"It's pulled away my trapdoor," said Kip.

A shadow fell over the pit. Then a long, black,
bristly, sticklike object descended into the hole. It
moved backward and forward, its tip searching for the
tunnel entrance.

"What is *that?*" gasped Lady Grant.

"That's one of its legs," said Frank. "Everybody—squeeze up tight against the wall!"

They huddled together, pressing themselves against the wall at the tunnel's end. The tip of the leg found the tunnel entrance and began to move slowly toward them, like a huge, hairy snake—and with it came the smell. A rancid, bitter smell of cockroach. There was a hooked claw on the end of the leg, and it scraped against the tunnel floor as it advanced.

Kitty whimpered.

"It's all right," said Prudence, putting a motherly arm around the girl's shoulders. "It can't reach us."

Measle wished he could believe that. The thing didn't seem to be stopping. The claw came closer and closer, weaving from side to side. Then, when it was only half an inch from the huddled bodies, it stopped. Slowly, carefully, it explored the sides, the floor and the ceiling of the tunnel. Then, suddenly, it retreated. As the cockroach pulled its leg out of the tunnel, it scraped it hard against the corner, where the tunnel met the pit, and a shower of wood splinters fell from the roof.

"That was too close for comfort," said Frank.

"You're right," said Kip. "We've got to dig some more."

The three men attacked the wooden face of the wall with every tool they had, and soon there was a growing pile of wood chips and sawdust. Measle, Prudence and Kitty pushed it all through the nearest hole in the floor. Lady Grant did nothing to help them; she just stared with wide eyes toward the pit at the beginning of the tunnel.

They dug for hours, lengthening the passage by a couple of inches.

"That'll do for the moment," said Kip, his face streaming with sweat and his hair gray with sawdust.

"We'd better cut another hole in the floor," said Frank. "We're going to need all the air we can get."

Cutting down through the remaining quarter inch of plywood took another hour. It was Kip who broke through.

"Hey—look at this," he said, peering down at the opening he'd made.

"What is it?" said Frank.

"Looks like an electric cable. But you're the expert, Frank. You tell me."

Kip moved aside to let Frank take a look.

"You're right," said Frank. "That's one of mine. I think it's the main power line that connects the control center to the train tracks. I reckon I can reach it." He lay down and pushed his arm through the hole. "Yup. It's right under us."

Kip tapped him on the shoulder. "You say it leads to the control box?" he said.

"Yup. Right up inside."

"And it's made of steel? The control box?"

"Yup. It's a steel box, screwed down into the plywood."

Kip thought for a moment. Then he looked somberly around at the group. "I think that's where we ought to be," he said. "Inside a steel box. Nothing—not the bat and not the roach—can get at us there."

"All this running about. Surely we're safe enough here?" said Lady Grant, not taking her eyes off the far end of the tunnel.

As she spoke, the black leg appeared again in the pit. This time, it made no effort to approach them. Instead, it maneuvered its hooked claw to the angle where the tunnel and the pit met. The claw dug deep into the tunnel ceiling and then pulled hard. It strained for a moment—and then there was a splintering sound as a section of the tunnel ceiling was ripped away. The claw withdrew, dragging the ragged piece of plywood with it. A moment later, it reappeared. Once again, the claw dug into the roof of the tunnel, strained and then yanked another section away.

"It's trying to dig us out," said Frank. "I didn't know roaches were so clever."

"That's no ordinary cockroach, Frank," said Prudence. "Basil's brain is in there, remember? He may be mad, but he can still think."

Kip took Lady Grant's small smooth hands in his huge rough ones and stared into her face. "Still believe we're safe enough here?" he said quietly.

"No, Mr. Lovell," whispered Lady Grant. "No, I don't."

They dug downward, enlarging the hole at their feet and trying to ignore the sound of splintering wood behind them. The cable was directly beneath them, perhaps half an inch below the bottom of the hole. When the hole was big enough, Frank said, "I installed it—I guess I should go first?"

There was no argument. Frank lowered himself into the hole, until only his head and shoulders were showing. "Got it," he said. "I'm touching it with my toes. If you men could grab my hands and lower me down a little farther——"

Kip and William took hold of Frank's arms and slowly let him down farther into the hole.

"Okay——I'm standing on it now," said Frank. "You can let me go. I'm going to drop down on my hands and knees."

Kip and William let go of Frank's hands and Frank disappeared from view. "It's good," he called. "Let me have the kids next."

William and Kip lifted Measle into the hole and slowly lowered him. Measle felt his ankles grabbed from below and then heard Frank's reassuring voice. "I've got you——you're almost there——just a little bit farther."

Measle's toes touched down on a solid surface, and a moment later, he was lying face down on a curved section of black rubber. Frank was kneeling beside him. He said, "Whatever you do, Measle, just don't look down. You're safe if you don't look down."

Measle looked down. He couldn't help it. His curiosity overcame his fear and he looked. Then he brought his head back quickly and closed his eyes. The floor was so far away and his position on the rounded top of the cable seemed so precarious that he suddenly felt dizzy. He dug his fingers into the hard black rubber surface and pressed his body as flat as it would go.

"Crawl along a little way, Measle," said Frank. "We've got to make room for the others."

Slowly, Measle inched himself forward along the cable. He knew, logically, that if he was careful, there was little danger of his falling. The cable was thick and strong and as wide as a double bed, but the fact that it curved away downward on either side of him was very disturbing and he was careful to stay in the exact center—and equally careful to hold on very tightly.

It took some doing—with a lot of terrified squealing from Lady Grant—but eventually everybody was lying prone along the cable. Prudence had stuffed Tinker into the front of her old jacket and done up the zipper, so that only his head was protruding. Kip was the last to lower himself down the hole and join them.

He brought with him both tool kits and his chain saw, all hanging from his broad leather belt. "Silly to leave them behind," he said. "We might need them again. Okay, Frank, lead the way."

Frank looked back over his shoulder. "Everybody take hold of the person's ankle in front of you and go really slowly."

They inched along the wire that stretched over the dizzying drop. Behind them, the sound of splintering wood grew fainter as they put distance between it and themselves. The underside of the table was close above their heads, and as they moved forward, it gradually got closer and closer, until Measle could feel the smooth plywood scraping on his back. In front of him, Frank stopped.

"Hold it," he said. "There's a staple up ahead. I remember putting it in to stop the cable from dangling. We've got to get around it somehow."

Measle lifted his head and peered over Frank's body. Just in front of Frank, the cable was fixed tight to the underside of the table with a steel staple. There seemed to be no way of getting past it. Frank crawled forward, his head bumping on the table. Measle watched as

Frank reached forward and grabbed the side of the staple. Then he did a very brave thing: he let his body slide to one side, so that he was hanging by his hands, his chest and legs dangling against the curved side of the cable.

"Oh—do be careful, Mr. Hunter," called Prudence from somewhere behind Measle.

Frank grunted. Then he began to swing his body from side to side. Each swing was wider than the last until, with one huge effort, he managed to pivot his legs past the staple and back up onto the cable on the far side. Still holding tight to the steel bar, he pulled the rest of his body up until he was once again lying flat on the curved rubber surface.

"Okay—here's what we're going to do," he called. "I'm going to help each one of you past this thing. You've just got to trust me. I won't let go. Kip, if you could come up to the front and help me with the heavier ones? Measle—you first. Grab my hand."

The dizziness swept over Measle again and for a moment he couldn't move. "Come on, Measle," said Frank. "Any kid who can do what you did out there by the lake can do this. Give me your hand."

Measle took a deep, shuddering breath and reached out his hand. He felt the cold metal of the staple—and then Frank's strong grip on his wrist. "Good boy," said Frank. "Now, just let yourself slide sideways. Don't worry—I've got you."

Measle swallowed hard, took another deep breath, closed his eyes and then shuffled his body to the right. He felt himself slipping over the edge—but Frank's grip on his wrist was like a bracelet of iron. Even as he started to slide down the curved surface of the cable, he felt himself being pulled upward. He kept his eyes tightly shut until he was sure he was back on solid rubber. Then, cautiously, he opened them. Frank was grinning at him.

"There—that wasn't so bad, was it?"

Kitty came next. Measle noticed that she seemed to have little fear and never closed her eyes for a second. She even smiled when she was dangling from Frank's hands and seemed almost to enjoy the whole experience.

"Weren't you scared?" he whispered, when she crawled next to him.

Kitty pointed to a badge on her uniform. "It's a

climbing badge," she said. "I've always been good at climbing."

One by one they all made it past the staple. Lady Grant screamed several times and Prudence (who was carrying the added weight of Tinker) had to be swung past the obstacle by both Frank and Kip, but neither she nor Tinker made any fuss at all and soon she was sitting safely on the other side of the staple, patting her gray hair back into place.

Kip was the last to come over and he needed no help, even with the heavy tool kits dangling from his belt. He imitated Frank and swung himself past the obstacle, using his great strength to haul himself up to safety.

Ahead of them, the cable looped down at a shallow angle and then looped up again, disappearing in the distance through a neat, circular hole cut in the plywood ceiling. The party dragged themselves forward, each person clutching the ankle of the one in front. It took them a long time and, when they at last reached the opening, they were all tired. On the final stretch, the upward slope of the cable meant that they had to pull themselves hand over hand, hauling themselves up the long black rubber hill until their arms ached with the effort. Prudence was the most exhausted of all of them and Kip, bringing up the rear, had to push against her feet to help her up the incline.

At last, they made it. One by one, they crawled up through the round hole and, once safely inside, they dropped off the cable and stood thankfully on solid ground.

The inside of the control box was a strange place. It was dark, apart from a few narrow beams of light that streamed through a wide mesh grille on one wall. Everywhere there were wires of different colors, running to connections over their heads. The still air smelled of oil and faintly of ozone. Kip knocked on one wall. "Solid steel," he said. "Nothing can get in here."

Lady Grant sat dejectedly in a corner, her head in her hands. "But we can't stay in here forever," she moaned. "We'll starve to death."

"We have to get rid of the roach," said Frank.

"Wait a minute," said William. "Won't the bat do that for us? Tonight, when it's out hunting? I bet that cockroach would make a great catch for it."

Frank had been peering out through the steel grille.

He said, "Come and take a look—we've got a grand-stand view from here."

They all clustered around the grille. Through the narrow bars, they could see, in the distance, the roof of the town hall and the tops of the trees in the square.

"If anything happens tonight," said Frank, "between the bat and the roach, I mean—we'll see it. I'll take the first watch."

8

THE
STEEL BOX

That night the bat came flapping once again in great circles over the tabletop. *Crack, crack, crack* went its wide leather wings. The group, woken from fitful sleep by the sound, pressed their faces against the grille. They could see the bat's huge shadow against the pale walls of the attic. They watched as it wheeled over the table and they saw it suddenly check its flight, seeming to hover for a moment before it dived straight for the town hall.

"It's seen the cockroach," said Frank.

152

The town hall was shrouded in darkness and at this distance they were unable to see what was going on. But they could hear, and what they heard was very strange. A great cacophony came from the town square: screeching and scratching and rattling and odd—and very unpleasant—high-pitched hissing that seemed to go on for several minutes.

"What's happening?" said Lady Grant. "Why doesn't it just grab the revolting thing and fly away?"

The reason the bat didn't simply take hold of the giant cockroach was this: inside the insect's brain was Basil's mind—and Basil was no fool, which made the cockroach that he'd become a lot smarter than the average cockroach. For the first time in his long and evil life, Basil was afraid—and what he was afraid of was his own little pet, Cuddlebug. He knew that Cuddlebug would never recognize his master in the black, shiny carapace of the cockroach. He knew that Cuddlebug would merely think he'd found the finest and largest meal of his life. So Basil had to find shelter. He smashed his way into the town hall, ramming his huge body through the center doors and bringing down most of the front wall and a good part of the ceiling with it. Even with this destruction, there was enough left of the town hall to shield him from the bat's talons. And, by turning his hard, shell-covered wing cases toward the shattered front of the building, Basil presented to his attacker a smooth, solid and unbreakable surface, which the bat—scratching and clawing as hard as it could—was unable to get hold of. The curved talons scraped and slid over the unyielding surface and Basil the roach kept his body pressed hard against the back wall of the room, clinging on with his claws and never budging an inch. All the while, he kept up a steady, high-pitched hissing.

"What's going on over there?" said William.

"Sounds like a fight of some sort," said Kip. "I think the bat is having problems."

Then there was silence. They stared through the grille, straining their eyes in the darkness. A moment later, they heard the *whoosh* as the bat took off and the *crack, crack, crack* of its wings fading into the distance as it flew through the broken window at the far end of the attic.

"Did it get it?" Prudence asked.

"Let's hope so," said William.

Then they heard shuffling and scraping, as if some great creature was shifting its body into a different position.

"I think I spoke too soon," said William. "I don't know how the cockroach did it—but I think it beat the bat."

Kitty was staring at the ceiling of the steel box. She said, "I bet I could get through that."

The rest of the group looked at her and then followed her gaze upward. Set into the top of the box was a series of narrow slots, and through them, they could just make out the rafters of the attic high above them.

"You silly girl," said Lady Grant. "Why would you *want* to get through it?"

"I bet I could see everything from up there."

"I bet you could," said Measle.

"And you're the only one who could squeeze through there, too. I certainly couldn't and that's a fact," said William.

Prudence shook her gray curls. "But my dear—what if it comes for you?"

"Well, I can get back in quickly if it starts coming this way," said Kitty.

"You're a real little trooper," said Frank. "Okay—but be careful."

Kip hoisted Kitty onto his broad shoulders. She reached out her hands and grasped the bars above her head. Then she stood upright on Kip's shoulders and he took hold of her feet and gently pushed her upward. Kitty wriggled her shoulders, then the rest of her body, through the one of the slots and, a moment later, was standing on the top of the control center.

"Oh, wow" they heard her say.

"What can you see?" said Kip.

"Everything" came back Kitty's voice. "I can see the whole layout from here."

"What about the town square?"

"Well, it's a bit dark—wait a minute—I can see the front of the building—it's all smashed in—some of the roof has fallen down—but there's something moving in there—something big and shiny—it's turning around—it's coming out—ooh, help! It's coming this way!"

Kitty's legs dropped down through the slot, and Kip stepped forward and grabbed her ankles and lowered her gently to the floor.

"It's the cockroach, all right," Kitty panted. "It doesn't look like it's hurt at all—and it's headed right here."

They all heard the sound of its pattering feet drawing closer and closer, and they all smelled the cockroach stink as it reached the steel box. Its huge shadow fell across the grille in the wall. There was a slithering, rasping sound as it pulled its body up onto the top of the control center and then its black belly flattened against the ceiling slots.

"It's right on top of us," whispered William.

"We're safe enough," said Frank. "But, to be safer still, let's get under there."

He pointed to the far wall. Some kind of electrical junction box stuck out from the side of the steel wall there, forming a low cave just beneath it. They ran across the space and crawled under the ledge, just as one long, hairy, black roach leg squirmed between the ceiling slots. They all pressed themselves tight into the small space. The claw on the end of the leg touched the ground in exactly the spot where they had just been standing. Then it scraped slowly across the floor, weaving back and forth, covering every inch of the floor in its search for them. It tapped against the protruding ledge—and

157

then curved around beneath the ledge and began to inch its way toward them.

Lady Grant moaned in terror, pulling her feet away from the approaching horror. As she did so, a shoe slipped off her left foot. Without thinking, she reached forward to snatch it—and Kip grabbed her by the waist and dragged her backward.

"But that shoe is a *Manolo*!" whispered Lady Grant. "Do you have any idea what they *cost*?"

"I don't care if it's a diamond the size of your head, lady!" muttered Kip. "Stay back!"

The claw scraped over the floor, searching this way and that, until it touched the shoe. It strained forward, the whole leg quivering with the effort—and then it hooked the shoe and pulled it back and up and out of sight.

"My lovely Manolo!" wailed Lady Grant.

"At least we know how far it can reach," said Frank. "And it can't rip its way in here."

For the rest of the night, Basil stayed pressed against the roof of the control center. Occasionally, he would push one of his legs through the slots and explore the interior of the box, while the humans inside huddled close together under the protective ledge. Toward dawn, he shifted suddenly, sliding with a thump off the steel box and then pattering away toward the town square.

"It knows the bat is coming back," said Frank. "It'll head for the town hall again."

Measle crawled out from under the ledge and the rest followed him. They made themselves as comfortable as they could and waited for daylight. Measle couldn't sleep. Another idea was forming in his head. He stared up at the coils of multicolored wires that draped and looped around the inside of the box. He didn't know anything about electricity, but there was someone there who did. He went over to Frank, who was leaning against the wall grille, his eyes shut.

"Frank? Are you awake?"

"I am now," said Frank, opening one eye.

"I was wondering—do you think it's possible to get the power on?"

"What—to the train set?"

"Yes."

Frank gazed up at the wires, his expert eyes flicking around at all the junctions and connections. "I suppose it could be done," he said at last. "It's just a question of rerouting a few lines. See that red cable? We could take a connection off that and then link it up to that black one over there—yeah, it can be done."

"What about making the trains move?"

"You want the trains to move? Why? Have you had another idea?"

"Well, I might have," said Measle. "But it all depends on the trains moving. Can you do that, too?"

Once again, Frank stared up at the lines of electrical cables. He didn't answer for some time and, all the while, his eyes were scanning the wires. At last, he said, "I think we could. We can't turn the spindles— they're too heavy for us—and those spindles control the train speed. That would mean that the trains would be going full tilt from the start—they'd probably come off the tracks on tight corners—but it's the best we could do."

"Could you control different trains?"

"Yes. Each one of those yellow wires goes to a different section of the track. All we have to do is patch in a temporary cable from there to there—one for each train—and we got it. So—what's the plan?"

"There's one more thing I need to know," said Measle. He pointed to the grille, set in the steel wall. "I'm going to have to get through there."

Frank examined the narrow bars of the grille and then looked at Measle. "Well, you're skinny—but not that skinny. Little Kitty might be able to do it, but not you."

"It has to be me," said Measle firmly. "Could we cut one of the bars?"

"It'll take some time," said Frank. "We've got two hacksaws between us, but this bar is pretty thick."

"But it could be done?"

"Yes, it could be done." Frank stared hard at Measle. "But before we start on something that's going to take a good two hours, I'm going to want to know why."

Measle sat down next to him and outlined his plan. As he did so, Frank's eyes got wider and wider, and when Measle finished he let out a big sigh and said, "It's out of the question."

"Why?"

"Because it's too dangerous, that's why."

"The mirror thing was dangerous, too, and you all let me try that."

Frank shook his head. "That was different," he muttered. "This time, there's a lot more that could go wrong."

"But you think it might work?"

Frank thought for a moment, his forehead creased in a frown. Then he said, "It's possible. It's completely crazy—but it's possible. But we can't let you do it. If anybody does it, it ought to be an adult."

"No," said Measle quietly. "It's got to be me. First of all, it'll take too long to cut enough of the bars to let an adult out—and, second of all, it's me that Basil wants. It's me he's furious at, not any of you. He just wants all of you back in your proper places. Me, he wants to kill."

"And that's why we can't let you do it," said Frank, closing his eyes and leaning his head back against the grille.

"What if we voted on it?" said Measle.

Frank sighed. "I guess you're going to tell them, aren't you? And I guess maybe some of them will *want* you to do it. Well, we live in a democracy, I suppose. And a democracy means that everybody gets a say. Okay—if you insist. We'll take a vote. But let me tell you right now—I'm going to vote no."

The vote was split right down the middle.

Frank, Kitty and Prudence were strongly against the idea. Kip, William and Lady Grant were for it. Kip and William were worried by the scheme, but they both agreed that there seemed to be no alternative. Lady Grant just moaned and said, "Anything! Anything to save us from that revolting monster!"

"Looks like we're stuck for a decision," said Frank. "You can't go unless there's a clear majority, Measle."

"What about me?" said Measle. "Don't I get a vote?"

"Of course you do," said William. "It's the democratic way."

"Well—I vote yes, too," said Measle.

"What a surprise," said Frank flatly.

There was a lot to do.

Kip and William began the long, tiring process of cutting through one of the bars on the steel grille. Their hacksaws were tiny compared to the thickness of the metal, and after an hour of solid work, they had only managed to cut halfway through one bar. Meanwhile, Frank was busy with the electrical system—cutting through the plastic coating on one wire, splicing another onto the exposed copper, rerouting a third in a long loop that ran clear across the box—and, all the time, humming softly under his breath as he worked.

Soon after daylight, the sawing work on the steel bar stopped when they heard a sudden loud buzzing that seemed to come from all around them.

"Power's on," said Frank. The smell of ozone was in the air, and already they could feel the interior of the box losing its nighttime chill. Frank dragged a length of red wire across the floor. "It could get pretty hot in here," he said.

It took another hour to cut through the bar, and by the time they were finished, Kip and William were sweating and William's hands had developed several blisters.

Frank pulled the red cable to one of a row of junction boxes set high on the wall. He took a sharp knife from his toolbox and stripped the plastic sheathing from the end of the wire, exposing the bright copper strands. "Okay," he said. "We're ready to go. All I've got to do is touch this cable end to one of these connections and you've got a train. Question is—which one?"

"Time for our lookout," said Kip. He hoisted Kitty onto his shoulders, lifting her up to the ceiling slots, and Kitty wriggled through the bars and onto the roof of the box.

"Where's the cockroach?" Kip called up to her.

"It's in the square. Right up next to the statue. It's not moving. No—wait a minute—it's waving its antenna things."

"Revolting," said Lady Grant, who had taken off her remaining shoe and was holding it close to her, as if it were a baby.

Kip turned to Measle. "Okay. We're all set, Measle. This is it."

"Please be careful, Measle," said Prudence.

Kip brought something out from behind his back. He held it out to Measle. "I think you might need this," he said. "Or rather, *we* might need it. It'll help us to see you. I just made it."

Measle took the object and examined it. It was a short length of wood with a small triangular red piece of cloth he'd ripped from his shirt nailed to one end.

"See," said Kip, "I thought if you could stick one end of that in your belt, we'd have a better chance of pinpointing your position. All we have to do is look for the flag."

Measle pushed the end of the stick into the back of

his trousers and tightened his belt. The flag hung at arm's length over the top of his head.

"Now," said Kip, "when you get outside, we should be able to see where you are."

Measle thought it was an excellent idea—he liked knowing that somebody would be following his progress. Somehow it made him feel just a little more secure. Frank was the only one who remained silent. Suddenly he stepped forward, frowning.

"I don't want you to do this, Measle. In fact, vote or no vote, I've changed my mind. I'm not going to let you do it. It's just too dangerous."

There was a long, awkward silence. Then William said, "Dear, oh dear. You sound like my boss. I thought this was a democracy?"

Frank nodded curtly. "It is. But somebody has to make responsible decisions. Measle's just a kid, for God's sake!"

Measle looked around the steel room, staring hopefully into each face for some show of support. But nobody wanted to meet his gaze. Their eyes slid away from his, some looking down at the floor, others peering up at the ceiling. Kip shook his head sadly and said, "He's right, you know, Measle. It's too risky. I know I voted to let you go——but I've changed my mind as well."

William said, "Yes. There must be another way. Sorry, Measle."

Kitty sniffed. "I never wanted you to do it," she whispered.

Measle looked at Lady Grant. She was sitting close to the wall, her hands limp at her sides, her legs stretched out in front of her. She met his eyes and Measle could see the indecision in her face. They looked at each other quite blankly for several seconds. Then she did a strange thing. She *winked* at him.

There was another long silence, as awkward as the first. Then suddenly——and without warning——Lady Grant screamed.

"Owwww! Owwww——that hurts! My hand! My hand!"

Everybody stared at her. Her eyes were tightly closed and her whole face was screwed up in a tight grimace of pain. Her right hand was hidden behind her back, and with her left, she was clawing frantically at the air. Prudence hurried over to her and squatted by her side.

"Whatever's the matter, dear?"

"My hand! It's got my hand! Make it let go! Owww! *Owww!*"

William and Kip knelt beside her. Frank bent over and grabbed her right arm.

"No! That hurts! Let me go!" shrieked Lady Grant.

Frank pulled again, more gently this time. "What's got your hand? There's nothing there, Lady Grant. Look—there's nothing there."

Lady Grant opened her eyes. "Isn't there? Really?" She smiled vaguely, looking around the steel box as if she wasn't quite sure where she was. Then, suddenly, her eyes narrowed.

She took a deep breath and yelled, "Now, Measle! *Now!*"

Frank whirled around. "No!" he shouted.

He was too late. While everybody's attention was elsewhere, Measle had been edging steadily toward the grille, and now he stepped up to the gap in the iron bars and, with one fluid movement, wriggled through.

"Measle! Wait!" shouted Frank, reaching out through the bars.

Kip put his hand on Frank's shoulder. "Let him go,"

he said. "We can't stop him now."

Frank turned and stared angrily at Lady Grant. "You shouldn't have done that," he said.

Lady Grant tilted her head to one side and shrugged. "You won't say that if he saves us," she said calmly.

Outside the safety of the steel box, Measle felt very alone and very exposed. He walked a little way, until he could no longer hear the others. Then he turned and looked back. Kitty was standing on the roof of the control center and she waved at him. Measle, feeling far from brave, waved back.

Inside the box, everybody was so intent on watching Measle through the grille that nobody noticed Tinker until it was too late. The little dog slipped away from Prudence, tore silently toward the grille and jumped with one bound onto Kip's back, over his head and through the hole they had cut. He barked with pleasure at his newfound freedom and raced toward Measle.

"No, Tinker!" whispered Measle. "Go back!"

Tinker took no notice. He wasn't going back into that strange dark box for anybody, not even for this nice smelly kid who was making shooing movements at him with his hands. He danced happily around Measle, his tongue lolling, his eyes rolling, yelping with joy— and suddenly Measle didn't feel quite so alone.

"Come on then, boy," he said. "Let's go and do what we've got to do."

He reached around his back and settled the stick into his waistband. The flag fluttered gently over his head. Then he took a deep breath and began to walk away from the control box.

9

THE ENGINE

In a wide arc around the control box, the tabletop had been left bare, but a foot away from the steel housing, the green-painted sandpaper began, and within another six inches, there was the start of the forest.

Measle set off across the tabletop, his heart thumping in his chest. Tinker, seeming to sense the importance of their mission, trotted quietly at his side. They moved as silently as possible between the trees, walking roughly in the direction of the town square.

171

Measle was trying as hard as he could to picture in his mind the entire layout of the train set. He concentrated particularly on the rail line that ran from the dirty railroad yard through the outskirts of town and into the forest. He reckoned that, if he and Tinker kept walking in a straight line, they should come across the tracks fairly soon—and moments later, there they were, gleaming in the morning light. He stepped onto the line and looked left and right. To his left, about two feet away, the tracks disappeared in a wide turn that Measle knew led back toward town. To his right, the tracks led away in a straight line for several feet, and Measle could see in the far distance the point where they met the very edge of the table. There the line made a sharp turn to the right, and Measle knew that the track ran alongside the edge of the table until, at the table's end, it made another wide arc before doubling back on itself.

"This is where we do it, Tinker," he said. "I just hope I can run as fast as you can. Come on."

They began to walk between the rail lines, stepping on each broad railway sleeper and avoiding the loose gravel that lay between them. Measle tried a short run.

Yes, it was possible to get quite a good speed up, leaping from sleeper to sleeper—until his foot slipped and he hit the gravel, instantly tripping and falling hard on the sharp stones. He sat there for a moment, pressing his scraped hands to his chest. Tinker stood quietly by his side, with a puzzled look on his face. *Is this part of the plan?* he thought. *Or is it because this nice smelly kid just isn't very good at running? Of course, four legs are better than two—stands to reason, doesn't it?*

Measle got to his feet and patted Tinker on the head, and they began to walk again.

They followed the line as it curved to the right. On either side, the trees seemed to press in against them. Once they had passed the long bend, Measle was relieved to see the dirty rail yard buildings in the distance. He could just make out the hulking shape of the big black locomotive, its huge cowcatcher sticking out in front like a set of buckteeth. The engine seemed to be crouching, ready to leap forward at a moment's notice.

They walked on and then, as Measle had expected, they came to a point where the forest thinned suddenly on the left-hand side of the tracks. Here Basil had left a broad open area in which he had set the logging camp. Small huts stood on either side of a muddy track. The logging mill itself was set by the side of the tracks and Measle could see the dusty machinery in its gloomy interior. Stumps of newly cut trees were everywhere, and one even had an ax head embedded deeply in it, the handle sticking up at an angle.

Measle and Tinker left the tracks and set off up the muddy trail, which was, of course, not muddy at all. It was perfectly dry, but Basil had scrunched up the sandpaper here and painted it brown, so that it looked like a rutted, potholed pathway through the woods. The track twisted this way and that, but most of the turns were to the right and Measle knew that, quite soon, they would reach the outskirts of the town.

"Can you see him?" Kip called up to Kitty, who was still standing on top of the box.

"I can see his flag," she called back.

"Where is he now?"

"He's almost at the edge of town—just coming out of the trees, along the dirt road."

"Good," called Kip. "Keep your eyes fastened on that

174

flag." He turned to Frank, who was standing by the row of connectors, the red cable in his hands. "Ready?" he said.

Frank nodded. "As ready as I'll ever be."

This is the hard part, Measle thought, as he and Tinker cleared the last of the trees and stepped into the edge of the town. *This is the part where luck has to take over.*

The houses here were cottages, all stuck together in a line on either side of the street. Each little house had a small front yard and in each yard stood the trash cans, two per house. They were the old-fashioned sort, made of galvanized, corrugated steel, each with a round lid that had a handle on top. Measle went to the nearest house and took the lids off two of the trash cans. He held them up like cymbals.

"I'm going make a lot of noise now, Tinker," he said.

This is it, he thought. *It's now or never.*

Measle raised the two steel lids high in the air, separating them as far as his arms could stretch. He swallowed once, gritted his teeth and then brought his hands together as hard as he could. The steel lids crashed together with a great clanging sound that seemed to bounce off the walls of the cottages, echoing back and forth between the houses.

Tinker dropped to the ground, his stubby tail between his legs. What was the smelly kid *doing*? Oh no—he was doing it again! *Crash! Clang! Smash! Bang!* Well—whatever it was, it looked like he was enjoying himself, so Tinker decided that this was all part of some new game. A musical game, perhaps? Tinker jumped to his feet, his tail high. He lifted his head and started to howl—a high-pitched, yodeling yell that mixed horribly with the discordant crashes of the steel lids. *Crash! Howl! Clang! Howl! Smash! Howl! Bash! Howl!*

In the town square, the cockroach's antennae turned.

Basil had suffered an unpleasant night. Being an insect was bad enough, but being attacked by his own little pet was an appalling state of affairs. And then he had spent a frustrating few hours trying in vain to get at that filthy little Measle, together with his little plastic victims who had—and this was the most infuriating and puzzling part of it all—somehow come back to life.

And now Basil was very, very hungry. He was also in

a savage fury and this clashing, crashing, banging sound somewhere at the edge of town was making his brain ache. Dimly, in his muddled mind, he realized that the noise was almost certainly being made by Measle, for only a dirty, filthy, sneaky boy could be causing such a racket.

Basil turned his great body so that he faced the direction from which the noise was coming. He waved his long antennae in the air, tasting the scent that blew in the slight breeze. Yesss! It was him! That foul little Measle—he should have disssposed of him years ago! Well, he'd disssspose of him now! He'd disssspose of him and eat him, sssstarting with his head and working his way ssslowly all the way down to his toes! And that would be the end of the filthy creature! Yesss—

Basil heaved himself forward and, with gathering speed, began to scuttle toward the sound.

Tinker smelled the cockroach before Measle saw it. The dog suddenly stopped howling and turned his nose in the direction of the town center. He crouched low, his stubby tail tucked between his hind legs, the wiry hair on his shoulders rising into a stiff crest and a low, rumbling growl sounding deep in his chest.

"What is it, boy?" said Measle, halting his lid bashing for a moment. Tinker growled again, his nostrils twitching. "Is it coming?" Measle asked, the pitch of his voice rising through fear. Tinker darted him a quick glance, as if to say, *Of course it's coming—can't you smell it?*

And then, rounding a corner at the end of the street, came the great black cockroach, its antennae waving furiously and all six legs pumping back and forth as it scuttled toward them. Measle dropped both steel lids to the ground with a crash and turned and fled, Tinker close behind him.

Inside the control box, all eyes were staring upward through the ceiling slots.

"What's happening, dear?" asked Prudence.

"I'm not sure," called back Kitty. "Could you hear the noise?"

They had all heard it. Tinker's howls and the crashing of the steel lids were far in the distance, but they had heard them quite clearly.

"Is there any movement?" called Kip.

"No, not yet—wait! The noise has stopped! Yes! I

can see the flag—it's starting down the muddy road—it's moving fast! And—and—the cockroach is chasing him!"

"Tell us when he reaches the railroad tracks!" shouted Frank, moving the hand holding the red cable a little nearer the row of connectors.

Measle and Tinker raced down the wide path. Behind them—and getting steadily nearer—was the pounding, scratching sound of the roach's claws. Sometimes they heard trees breaking and falling as the great insect bulldozed its way toward them.

By the time they reached the railway tracks, Measle was panting with exhaustion. He reckoned that the cockroach was just now reaching the far edge of the logging village—which meant that, at its present rate of speed, the monster would be on them in about fifteen seconds. Measle made a quick decision. He risked five of those precious seconds to reach behind him and grab the stick in his belt. He pulled it clear and waved it frantically, reaching up as far as he could, the little red flag fluttering wildly in the air.

Kitty screamed.

"He's at the tracks! He's waving the flag! The cockroach is— Oh, no! The cockroach is almost there! Wait! Measle's moving again! He's moving fast down the tracks! The cockroach is right behind him!"

"Now!" shouted Kip.

Frank touched the exposed end of the red cable to the first yellow wire. Kip looked back toward the ceiling slot. "Is there a train moving?" he shouted.

There was a pause. Then Kitty called down, her voice desperate. "It's the wrong one! It's the little freight engine! And it's going *backward*! Try a different one!"

Frank moved the red wire to the next yellow one in line.

"What now?" called Kip.

Another pause—and then Kitty's voice, breaking with panic. "No! No, not that one! That's the passenger train! And it's on the far end of the table! Do another one!"

Frank touched the cable end to the third wire.

Measle's legs felt like lumps of hot lead. The effort of running across the sleepers and avoiding the gravel in between them was enormous. The tracks stretched out in front of him, as straight as an arrow to the far table edge. Measle knew that there were, in fact, only a few feet between him and the sharp curve at the end, but it looked like a mile at least and he wasn't sure he could make it. He pounded on, his heart thumping in his chest, his feet slapping down on each sleeper in turn. Tinker ran beside him, occasionally throwing a look backward and growling deep in his throat. The roach was on the tracks now and, by the steadily increasing volume of its scraping claws against the iron rails, it was gaining on them rapidly.

Measle knew he wouldn't make it. It was too far to the edge of the table. He was too tired. And where was the great locomotive? It should be moving by now. It should be on the very tracks they were running along. He should be able to hear it. But he could hear nothing, except his own rasping breaths, his feet *slap-slap-*ping on the railroad ties and the terrifying sound of scraping and scrabbling and scratching and hissing—all too close behind him.

Then, out of the corner of his eye, he saw Tinker skid to a stop. He ran on a few paces and then halted himself. He turned and saw Tinker racing back along the track, straight toward the great insect.

"No!' he yelled. "Tinker! Come back!"

But Tinker didn't come back. Tinker had had enough. More than enough. All this running around and making loud noises was all very well—but no self-respecting *dog* was going to allow himself to be chased by a *bug*! It might be the size of a house with huge, nasty, dangerous-looking hooky, fangy thingies in its mouth—but what did that matter? It was just a bug, a stupid old bug! *And,* Tinker thought, *I am a dog, and dogs aren't scared of bugs. And now the smelly kid is yelling something—probably telling me to go for it! Right—I'll go for it! I'll show the smelly kid what I'm made of! Okeydokey—let's start with the growly-snarly-show-the-old-toothies routine, shall we?*

And Tinker, his lips pulled back in what he hoped looked like the most savage of savage snarls, bunched the muscles of his short back legs and accelerated toward the giant cockroach. For a moment, faced with the onrushing dog, Basil forgot what he was and felt a moment of fear. He'd always hated dogs. They scared him. Those teeth! That noise they made whenever they saw him! And now here was this dog racing toward him, snapping and snarling and frothing at the mouth. Basil stopped, his huge claws skidding across the railroad sleepers and crunching against the gravel. Tinker stopped, too. He lowered his head and snarled, showing off his white teeth. Basil did nothing for a moment. Several feet down the track, Measle watched as the dog-sized Tinker and the whale-sized insect warily stared at each other.

Then Basil remembered what he was. He was a giant cockroach! This tiny creature couldn't hurt him! Its little teeth were no match for his great curved mandibles! Its soft skin couldn't compete with his hard shell! Any damage that was going to be done would be done by him! Basil lunged forward—and Tinker neatly sidestepped the great roach and circled around to its side, barking furiously. Basil heaved his huge body around to face the dog and lunged forward again. Again, Tinker jumped out of reach. Slowly, they circled each other, Basil moving ponderously forward, his curved jaws snapping, and Tinker jumping at the last second out of reach of the attacks and barking continuously.

In the control box, Frank had almost run out of wires. He'd tried almost all of them and, each time, Kitty, her voice rising into hysteria, had called down that it was the *wrong train*! And now there was only one connector left to try.

"It's got to be this one," he muttered. "It's just *got* to be!"

He touched the red cable end to the last of the connectors.

Measle had seen enough. It looked like Tinker was well able to fend for himself and this was an opportunity to get to where he wanted to go. He ran down the track, toward the distant table edge. Behind him he heard Tinker's barking and the cockroach's furious hissing dwindle as he raced away. Where the railway tracks met the edge of the table, they made a hard turn to the right, and this was where he would make his stand. If only the train would come!

He felt it long before he saw it. He was standing near the edge of the vast table, with one foot resting against the left rail. As he watched the distant battle—

Tinker still leaping nimbly away from Basil's attacks, Basil heaving his massive body around to face the dog again—he became aware of a slight tingling vibration in his toes. He looked down. The rail looked the same, and yet he could feel it distinctly now: a trembling, a faint pulsation, which quivered through his foot, into his ankle and up his leg. He dropped to his knees and put one ear to the cold steel, and there was a thrumming in his head that grew steadily louder and louder and louder. And there, far away up the railway tracks, just rounding the gentle curve, came the great black locomotive with its three dusty Pullman carriages, its pistons pounding, its wheels a blur and its massive cowcatcher skimming the rails toward him.

Tinker and the gigantic insect were too busy sparring with each other to notice what was bearing down on them, and Measle saw that, unless he did something fast, there was a good chance that Tinker would be hit by the train. He put his fingers in his mouth and blew a piercing whistle. Tinker jerked his head in Measle's direction.

What does he want, that smelly kid? Can't he see I'm busy here? And there's that whistling noise again! Does that mean he needs me? Maybe it's time to go—this fight's getting a bit boring—and now there's a funny noise, too—it's getting louder and louder—it's a bit scary, this funny noise—and now it's getting so loud that it's not so funny after all! And that means—Yip! Time to go—

Measle saw Tinker suddenly leave the battle and race toward him, his ears flattened, his legs stretching out in a breakneck gallop. The giant roach turned as well and begin to scuttle after Tinker, its six legs pumping back and forth as it gathered speed. And behind the roach came the great, smoke-belching, wheel-screaming, piston-packing, rail-rattling locomotive. . . .

Measle stood perfectly still. There was nothing left for him to do. Whatever was going to happen would happen now without any interference from him—just as long as the cockroach stayed on the tracks.

But Tinker, tiring of running across the railroad sleepers and scratching his paws on the gravel between them, veered suddenly sideways, running off the tracks and onto the painted grass at the side. The great cockroach veered away, too, off the tracks and out of danger—out of danger from the black, pointed cowcatcher on the front of the huge locomotive.

Measle started to yell, jumping up and down in the middle of the rail lines, waving his red flag as hard as he could, frantically trying to get the roach's attention away from Tinker and onto himself—

—and Basil saw the red flag, and under it the nasty, dirty, leaping figure of the boy, the boy he hated far more than he hated any stupid little dog. The boy was jumping up and down in the middle of the tracks. Basil forgot about chasing the stupid little dog and changed direction again, scrambling back onto the rail lines. Now he was almost there and he could see in his muddled mind's eye how he was going to flatten the filthy boy, flatten him and eat him, starting with the top of his head and working his way to the soles of his feet—he was almost there—

—and just as Basil reared his huge body forward to squash Measle flat, Measle hurled himself to one side, off the tracks and onto the painted grass at the side, rolling sideways as he landed until his body thumped against the trunk of a tree. Basil could not shift direction as fast as that. In a straight line, he could get up a terrific speed but the great mass of his cockroach body could never perform an agile move like Measle's, so he merely slowed down his forward pace and laboriously began the process of shifting his great body sideways off the track.

He was too late.

The massive cowcatcher on the front of the locomotive—skimming half an inch above the rails—slammed into him, catching his body from underneath and flipping it high in the air. Measle watched as the huge cockroach turned end over end, spinning upward toward the attic ceiling. He felt the blast of wind as the locomotive shrieked by. The locomotive, going at full speed now, hit the sharp turn and rocked violently from side to side, its small front wheels grabbing at the bending rails. Then the entire engine seemed to leap a foot in the air as it left the tracks, hurtling straight ahead over the edge of the table. It hit the attic wall with a deafening crash, followed by three successive crashes as the Pullmans hit as well. He looked up again and saw that Basil's spinning, upward flight was slowing down, and any moment he would begin the inevitable descent back toward the tabletop. In that split second Measle realized with a sudden flash of horror that Basil wouldn't fall over the edge of the table as he'd hoped. The cowcatcher had flipped Basil straight up in the air and not sideways at all, which meant that Basil would land back on the tabletop—and Measle knew that, no matter how high you dropped a cockroach, its hard outer shells always protected it from harm.

High in the rafters, Cuddlebug stirred. There was so much *noise* down there. Far more noise than usual. Crashing and smashing and bashing. This noise was very disturbing to a bat's sleep. Very disturbing indeed. So disturbing, in fact, that—

Cuddlebug opened one eye.

And here was dinner.

It was very strange. Dinner had never come to him before. He always had to seek dinner out. *Find* dinner. *Catch* dinner. And only then, *eat* dinner. And yet, here was dinner, spinning up toward his roost in a very peculiar flight pattern indeed, and it looked just like that large, juicy cockroach that had given him such trouble only a few hours ago. Who knew that cockroaches could fly? And since when did a bat eat its dinner in broad daylight? And who cared? Opportunities like this were rare.

Lazily, Cuddlebug reached out one enormous talon and grabbed Basil neatly out of the air.

And then the cockroach spell wore off.

It didn't happen all at once. The only evidence that the spell had run its course was that the cockroach, held firmly in Cuddlebug's grasp, began to get heavier. The bat's first reaction was *Ooh, great! A fatter dinner!* But then the weight began to be a burden. Basil's insect body started to swell, so that Cuddlebug's talon began to ache under the strain of holding it—and then the weight became so much that the bat's other talon, which was holding fast to the beam above it, began to slip away—and then Cuddlebug lost his grip on the beam entirely, and together he and Basil began to fall toward the tabletop—instinctively the bat spread his great leathery wings, which turned his downward fall into a glide—but dinner was getting too heavy and too fat and it was somehow changing shape in Cuddlebug's grasp, so Cuddlebug brought his other talon into play and now grasped the body with both sets of claws— yes, he had a better grip now—but his glide path was dropping fast, and he made a wide circle over the table- top, looking for somewhere that would give him much-needed height again—ah! The open attic window! If he could only get through there in time, before gravity completely overcame him! The bat flapped his huge wings frantically and flew quickly toward the broken window, gaining just enough height to clear, by an inch, the shards of dirty glass that stuck up from the base of the window frame like jagged spears. Cuddlebug shot out into the open air—and oh! The daylight! Too bright! His eyes! He was blind! Which way to turn? In his confusion and sudden blindness, Cuddlebug forgot everything he ever knew about flying and dinner and the effects of gravity, and as Basil's insect body grew and stretched and softened and changed its shape back into its human form, Cuddlebug, flapping furiously in crazy circles, suddenly lost his battle with the pull of gravity and began to plummet toward the distant ground.

Instinctively, Cuddlebug opened his claws and released his burden.

And in that moment, Basil was Basil again. He felt the sudden slackening of the grip—the grip of his beloved pet that had carried him safely, until this very instant, through the air—he felt the wind whistling past his face—he glimpsed the ground rushing up to meet him—

Basil had instincts, too.

Basil's instinct was to grab at something—anything!—just so long as it would stop this headlong plunge. He grabbed and clung tightly to the only objects within his reach. To the talons that had just let him go.

Cuddlebug shrieked a batty shriek of fear and fury and flapped his leathery wings as hard and as fast as he could. But it was no use. Gravity was winning this battle—and winning it in a spectacular fashion.

It was a long way from the attic window to the hard concrete pavement far below. Basil, now fully returned to his Wrathmonk self, no longer had his hard outer cockroach shell to protect him. And Cuddlebug had always been soft—on the outside, at least.

Measle saw none of this, but he could hear it all. From somewhere beyond the attic window, he heard three sounds. Cuddlebug's shriek of terror was at too high a pitch for human ears to hear, so the first sound to reach Measle's ears was Basil's long, howling scream as he plummeted to earth. The other two came a moment later.

SPLAT! And then, a second later——Splat!

Measle closed his eyes. His back hurt from where he'd rolled against the tree. He lay still for a moment. Then he felt something wet on his face, something wet and warm. He opened his eyes. Tinker was crouching over him, licking his face.

Tinker was getting bigger.

10

THE FALL OF THE HOUSE OF TRAMPLEBONE

Measle could see that Tinker was getting bigger because the surrounding scenery seemed to be shrinking. Where, moments before, the nearby trees had loomed over the dog, now Tinker was fully half their height. His legs straddled the entire width of the railway tracks, which seemed to be getting smaller and smaller—and yet Tinker didn't seem to be getting bigger in relation to *him*. Which meant—

He was growing, too.

Measle glanced around. Yes! His head was now

higher than the trees. He could look out over the forest—he could see the entire tabletop—and over there, the control box looked as if it was lifting itself clear off the surface of the table. He watched as the screws holding the box down on the plywood sheets were wrenched out of their holes with the sound of tearing wood. With a pop, the box was thrown to one side and he could see a very squashed-looking group of people crawling out of its shadow. And they were growing! Growing fast! And now his own arm brushed against the forest and thirty trees were demolished! He sat up quickly and felt the table wobble beneath him— he heard the creak as his weight increased—he saw Tinker suddenly stagger as the table shifted, then move away from him and jump toward the attic wall, landing with a thump on the floor. He looked again toward the people. They were close now, just a few feet away. Frank and Kip were grinning, and Lady Grant, still clutching her precious shoe, had tears running down her face, and William and Kitty and Prudence were jumping up and down and hugging one another, which was a bad idea because what with that and all their combined and rapidly increasing weights, the trestles supporting the great tabletop suddenly gave way and the whole vast expanse of plywood pancaked down to the floor with a great dusty crash.

It was lucky that Tinker was so agile. He had been sniffing around under the table at some tiny fragments of sawdust—some of which smelled like the smelly boy, some of which smelled like the little girl and all of which smelled like those metal things in the men's tool bags—and he'd heard a creaking sound over his head. He had looked up just in time to see the plywood sheets sagging toward him. He'd jumped out of the way just as the tabletop smashed down—onto the very spot where he'd been standing. And now, after all that excitement, there was the smelly boy, sitting in the ruins of the train set, looking a bit dazed but otherwise fine. Tinker trotted up and gave him a quick lick (partly out of friendship but mostly because he tasted good). And there, also sitting in a pile of wrecked miniature houses, was his dear old lady, rubbing her hip with one hand and picking bits of plaster out of her hair with the other, and she deserved a lick, too—as did all the other people, all of whom seemed a little dazed and confused, but that was all right, because the surroundings

196

had certainly changed dramatically and, as far as Tinker was concerned, for the better.

Measle began to crawl through the wreckage toward the others, but something was in his way. A rectangular block of stone, which hadn't been there a moment before, was suddenly blocking his view. He stood up, his feet crushing the entire logging camp, and began to walk around the block. But the block was getting bigger, expanding in all directions, left, right, and upward. Measle looked up and realized that it was the statue from the town square. Already the figures of the man and the woman were high above his head, just as they had been when both he and the statue were tiny. He looked around to see if anything else from the train set was growing—but no. It was just the statue on its stone base, rearing up now toward the rafters.

And then the straining floorboards creaked ominously.

On the other side of the statue, Kip was scrambling to his feet. He hauled Prudence up onto hers and shouted, "Quick, everybody! The floor won't take the weight! We've got to get out of here!"

Measle met them all at the attic door. "What's happening?" he shouted, over the sound of protesting timbers.

"I don't know!" yelled Kip. "But I do know wood, and this floor is going to give way any second now! Come on, everybody! Down the stairs and out of this house!"

They ran, stumbling down the stairs. Tinker was everywhere—under their feet, in front one minute, behind the next, barking with excitement. Down, down they went, first to the top landing, then down the main stairs—one flight, another flight—and all the time they could hear the attic floor groaning with the enormous weight that was resting on it. As they reached the hall at the foot of the stairs, a piece of plaster from the ceiling high above crashed to the floor, shattering over the filthy carpet.

"Out! Everybody out!" screamed Kip.

Frank wrenched open the front door, and they all piled out of the house and into the road, with Tinker dancing among them. When they had reached the safety of the opposite pavement, they turned and looked back toward the house. For a moment, everything appeared to be normal—or as normal as the grim house could ever look, with its soot-encrusted walls and its tall, fingerlike chimneys and its black-painted windows—and then, with a thunderous crash, the attic floor gave way and the great stone block, with the two statues on the top, began to fall through the house. It hit the floor beneath the attic as loudly as a bomb going off. That floor gave way instantly and the block continued on its way, smashing through the floor below, then on through the floor below that, and finally down to the street level, where it landed on the filthy carpet with an earsplitting *thump*.

And then the grim house did a very odd thing. It *sighed*. They could all hear it clearly—a great, sad exhalation of breath, as if it had lost the will to go on standing.

The chimneys were the first to go. Slowly, one toppled, then another and another, their sooty bricks crashing through the black slate roof. The roof shuddered and then collapsed inward and downward, ripping its way through what was left of the floors. The walls were last. They started to crumple, slowly at first, falling in on themselves with increasing speed until, with a roar, the whole building disappeared in an enormous cloud of black dust.

The dust blew over them. It smelled of dead fish, old mattresses and the insides of ancient sneakers. Everybody held their noses until the dust cloud settled— everybody except Tinker, who couldn't hold his nose and even if he'd been able to wouldn't have. To Tinker, there were no really bad smells. Just *interesting* ones.

Where the house had stood was a huge pile of black rubble. In the middle of the rubble stood the statue. The stone base was buried in the fallen bricks and roof slates, but the figures of the man and the woman stood clear above the wreckage.

Measle, his throat dry from the dust, croaked, "What happened?"

William began to say, "Beats me," but he only got as far as *Beats*—before Kip grabbed his arm and pointed at the statue. The outer stone on the two figures was cracking like an eggshell. A large chunk fell off the man's head, followed by another from the woman's outstretched arms. More and more cracks appeared on the figures, and more and more of the stone covering fell away—revealing to everybody's astonished eyes a *real* man and a *real* woman underneath. Suddenly, the man shook himself and the last of the stone fell away from his body. He reached down and began picking the remaining pieces from the woman's body, until both were free. Then he held out his hand and the woman took it. He lifted her from her knees and they clung to each other for a moment. Then they both turned and looked toward the group of people on the other side of the street.

They smiled. The man, still holding tightly to the woman's hand, stepped down onto the rubble, and together they picked their way over the ruins and walked across the road. When they reached the group, they stood first in front of Frank. The man let go of the woman's hand and took Frank's instead. He shook it and said, "Thank you." The woman reached up and kissed Frank on the cheek and she said, "Thank you," too.

They went to each person in turn, the man shaking hands, the woman kissing cheeks. When they got to Tinker, the man fondled the dog's ears and the woman knelt down and hugged him hard, pressing her lips against his rough muzzle.

They left Measle for last.

Measle had been staring hard at the man and the

woman, who were now standing in front of him. There was something about them both, something he could almost, but not quite, put his finger on. They looked familiar in some way, as if he'd known them a very long time ago. Old friends, perhaps, from a distant past. Very *good* old friends. The man was tall, with curly brown hair. His eyes were brown and they wrinkled at the corners when he smiled. They were wrinkling now. The woman was slim, her reddish hair tumbling over her shoulders. Her eyes were green, with tiny flecks of gold in them. She was very pretty. She was smiling, too. Measle stuck out his hand.

"Hi," he croaked. "I'm Measle Stubbs."

"No, you're not," said the man. "Your name isn't Measle Stubbs. It's Sam Lee Stubbs. I'm your dad and I should know."

"And I'm your mother," said the woman, and Measle looked at her and saw that even though she was smiling as broadly as the man, she was crying. She wiped her hand across her eyes, sniffed and said, "And you need a *bath*."

There were questions and explanations—and more questions and more answers—and a lot of hugging and

kissing, and Measle found himself unable to say anything very much because his heart was thumping in his
chest and he felt like crying, although he didn't know
why. He just stood and stared and grinned at the man
who was his father and the woman who was his mother
and, between answers and explanations, his father and
his mother stood and stared and grinned at him. At
last, in a pause in the babble, he tugged at the man's
sleeve and said, "Sam Lee?"

"That's your name," said Mr. Stubbs. "The name we
gave you when you were born. It's a mixture of our
names, your mother's and mine. I'm Sam Stubbs. Your
mother's name is Elizabeth but everybody calls her
Lee. The Wrathmonk called you 'Measle' because
Wrathmonks like to muddle things up. He used all the
same letters as 'Sam' and 'Lee,' but he mixed them
around and came up with 'Measle.' It was one of his
many ways of trying to hurt you."

Measle thought for a moment. Then he said, "Well,
it didn't work. I don't mind Measle. I've sort of gotten
used to it."

"Well," said Mr. Stubbs, "if you like being called
Measle, then we'll call you Measle."

"Thank you very much," said Measle. Something funny was happening to his eyes. They seemed to be watering quite badly. He blinked hard to make the wetness go away. To change the subject (and because he really wanted to know), he said, "Basil told me that you were killed by a deadly snake—and that wasn't true, was it?"

Mr. Stubbs raised one eyebrow. "You don't think so?" he said, a small smile turning up the corners of his mouth.

"Well, Basil never lied," said Measle. "At least, not as far as I know."

Mr. Stubbs nodded. "No, he never did. And he didn't lie about what happened to us, either. Of course, there were a few things he left out of the story. Things like the snake just happened to belong to *him*. And far from being alive, it was very, very *dead*. And it wasn't even a complete snake, just an ancient, mummified snake's head. An ancient mummified snake's head that had once wriggled about on Medusa's skull—"

"Who?" said Measle.

"Medusa. The Gorgon. Never heard of her?"

Measle shook his head. Mr. Stubbs turned to Mrs.

204

Stubbs and muttered, "Not just a bath, dear. Also an *education*." He turned back to Measle and grinned. "Well, son—Medusa was a very nasty monster who lived thousands of years ago. She was reasonably normal-looking, as far as monsters go, except for the fact that instead of hair, she had a whole lot of horrible snakes writhing about on her head. I don't know how she ever got any sleep with all that wriggling and hissing. Anyway, if you just *looked* at Medusa, you turned to stone. One peep at her ghastly face and bang! You were granite. Anyway, to cut a long story a bit shorter—"

"Oh, please don't," said Measle, who was enjoying the tale.

"Well, I'll give you the full version later. The important part is that Basil had somehow got hold of one of her mummified snakes' heads—as you can imagine, they're pretty rare objects these days—and that's what he used on us. Even dead and mummified and not even part of Medusa's scalp anymore, it still had a bit of power left. Not enough to petrify us all the way through, but just enough to give us a good thick covering of stone, and all before we could say,

'What's that you've got in your hand, Basil?' So you see, he was *sort of* telling the truth the whole time."

Measle wanted to hear a lot more about Gorgons and snakes and being turned to stone, but Mrs. Stubbs suddenly looked up at the sky and said, "It's getting late, dear. I do think we ought to be getting home."

"Home?" said Measle hopefully.

"Home," said Mr. Stubbs. "It's a nice big house, out in the country. Lots of land. A couple of streams, a little lake. It should still be there. I mean, only houses like this one fall over just like that. Why don't we go and see?"

Mrs. Stubbs had started to stroke Measle's head. Measle found that he rather liked his head being stroked. She bent down to him and said, "Come on, Measle. Why don't we go and see?"

"Okay," said Measle, wondering if anybody else could hear the thumping of his heart.

Mr. Stubbs turned to the others. "All of you lost a lot in there. A few years out of your lives, for a start. I'd like to help you out, if you'll let me. In the meantime, a few days of rest and relaxation won't do any of you any harm. So I want you all to come and stay with us for a while. There's plenty of room and you can stay as long as you like—until you get back on your feet."

Lady Grant limped forward, holding her remaining shoe tight against her chest. "Speaking of feet—this is so kind of you, Mr. Stubbs. Unfortunately, as you can see, I've lost one of my precious Manolos. It's somewhere underneath that *revolting* rubble. So I won't be able to walk very far."

Mr. Stubbs smiled. "Well, we shall have to do something about that, won't we? Just a moment."

He turned away and took a couple of steps along the pavement, separating himself from the group. He seemed to be thinking for a moment, his forehead creased in a small frown. Then his face cleared and he smiled to himself. "Funny how quickly things come back to you," he muttered. He raised his head, closed his eyes and said, quite softly, *"Cathalme stribenrallo Manolo carfax."*

"What did he say?" said William.

A small, delighted scream from Lady Grant made everybody's head swivel in her direction. Lady Grant, still clutching her right shoe, was staring down at her feet. Both were still bare, but right beside the big toe on her left foot stood a battered and dusty, left foot, high-heeled black shoe.

Mr. Stubbs grinned at her and said, "A bit bashed about, I'm afraid, but at least no longer buried."

"Oh dear," said Prudence, in a nervous voice. "Oh dear, oh dear, oh dear. Come along everybody, I think we ought to go now. *Right* now, in fact."

Mrs. Stubbs smiled around at them. "It's all right," she said. "He was just doing a little magic."

Prudence smiled weakly. "That's what I'm afraid of, Mrs. Stubbs. I mean to say—with all due respect— what exactly is your husband?"

"He's a Wizard, Miss Peyser. That was half the trouble, you see."

"Half the trouble?"

"As far as Basil Tramplebone was concerned. But that's another story. Don't worry. My husband is a very minor Wizard."

"Oh dear. But surely you'd rather keep that a secret? I mean, we—um—we ordinary mortals aren't really supposed to know he's a Wizard, isn't that so, Mrs. Stubbs?"

"Well," said Mrs. Stubbs confidentially, "I think it's

probably best that you do know. After all, you've been through so much. You've known a *Wrathmonk*, for goodness' sakes. What's a minor Wizard after that? And he's very nice, honestly he is. He wouldn't hurt a fly—unless, of course"—and here Mrs. Stubbs lowered her voice to a whisper—"unless of course the fly happened to be a *Wrathmonk*."

Mrs. Stubbs smiled a little, secretive smile at Prudence. It was the kind of smile that said, *You know what I'm talking about, don't you?* Then she looked around and frowned in disgust.

"And now, do let's get away from this horrible place as quickly as we possibly can."

Nobody said no, which was hardly surprising. The only remark spoken at all during the next few moments was by Prudence. She whispered into Lady Grant's ear, "*Minor* Wizard indeed! I don't think so, Lady Grant. Rather *major*, I would say."

"Really?" said Lady Grant, beaming with the prospect of mixing with members of the mystical elite. She detached herself from Prudence, put on her most winning smile and made a beeline for Mr. and Mrs. Stubbs. But before she could say a single flattering thing to them, Mrs. Stubbs had taken one of Measle's hands and Mr. Stubbs had taken the other and the three of them led the small group away from the dismal street forever.

When everybody had gone and the street was once again deserted, the small black cloud floated over the rubble, looking for something to rain on. Off to one side, at the edge of the ruined house, were two patches of green slime, one very small, the other quite large. There was something about those two patches of green slime that felt right to the small black cloud, so it positioned itself directly above them and began to release its rain.

The rain fell heavily and, quite soon, the two patches of slime began to dissolve, mixing with the black dust and the water into a soupy puddle. Soon the puddle slid into the gutter at the side of the road, slipped silently down a slight slope and, meeting a drain set into the channel, gurgled down into the darkness of the sewers.

And the small black cloud squeezed the very last of the water out of itself and then, with nothing left to rain on, popped—with the sound of a cork being pulled from a bottle—out of existence.

IAN OGILVY

is a writer and an actor. He's done more acting than writing, and most of that in England, where he was born. He's appeared in films, plays, and many television shows. MEASLE AND THE WRATHMONK is his first children's book. He lives in southern California with his wife, his two stepsons, and lots of dogs.